MW00653232

The Adventures of Lew and Charlie

By Maurice Decker

Trap Lines of Rat Lake Club
January 1926

The Fur Pocket on Big Thunder
August 1926

Trap Lines on Big Thunder
February 1927

Second Edition

ISBN 978-0-936622-31-6

CONTENTS:

INTRODUCTION:

Lew & Charlie are two stand-up guys who rely on their outdoor skills to survive in the wilderness hunting, trapping and fishing. They also solve mysteries, catch crooks, and rescue damsels in distress. Perhaps best described as an old-fashioned adventure serial, the stories ran uninterrupted for 35 years in *FUR-FISH-GAME* magazine, beginning with Trap Lines of Rat Lake Club in 1926.

Over the years, Maurice Decker wrote 36 novella-length Lew & Charlie adventures, all broken into monthly chapters with cliff-hanger endings. The last appeared in the December 1961 issue of *FUR-FISH-GAME*.

In 1985, to mark the magazine's 60th anniversary year, the editor decided to revise and republish one of the stories in its entirety, as 11 monthly chapters. When that story was coming to a close, readers who had become hooked on Lew & Charlie flooded the magazine office with letters asking for another story. Due to the outpouring of requests and enthusiasm, the adventure serial was revived and continues to be a favorite of many readers of *FUR-FISH-GAME*.

Those who don't like waiting a month between chapters have long asked for a Lew & Charlie book. But the stories never were published as anything other than monthly magazine installments—until now.

For this, the first Lew & Charlie book, we went back to the beginning, to the first stories, two of which never have been reprinted. Regular readers should enjoy meeting Lew & Charlie as young men embarking on their first outdoor adventures. But, really, anyone who enjoys a bold tale may have a hard time putting down this book.

– Jeff Kirn, Publisher

Trap Lines of Rat Lake Club
Chapter 1 – It's a Bet!

It all started one evening down in our "Club House" on Muskrat Lake. A bunch of us met there every few nights to swap hunting, trapping and fishing stories, true and untrue. Lew and Charlie were talking about taking a trapping trip up in some of the northern states that border on Canada. Both lamented the dearth of fur in our own neighborhood.

"No chance at all for a fellow around here anymore," said Lew. "Gosh, those birds up in the bush country sure are lucky."

"Why couldn't we have been born up there?" added Charlie. "It would be better than sitting around here, with nothing to trap except a few skunks."

I stood their prattle as long as I could, and then I spoke right up and said, "You guys don't know when you're well off. Why, a man can step out right here in this settled country and make as much money, clear money I mean, as you fellows would do if you went up in that northern country. Why, I don't pretend to be any wizard with the steel trap, but I'll bet I can make more right at home than you could in any of that God-forsaken land you're talking about."

Both Lew and Charlie looked pityingly at me and sadly shook their heads. "You always did get those funny notions," Charlie said.

This made me half mad.

"All right," I came back. "How much money do you want to put up on it? You fellows pack your duffle and hit the train for northern Minnesota or Wisconsin, anyplace you've been talking about, and I'll stake me out a line right here at home, within five to ten miles of the city limits. When you get your fill of being starved and half-froze, you beat it back home, bring your furs, and we'll have a reckoning. I've got an even hundred dollars your pile won't be twice as big as mine."

"Make it just as big," Birchy spoke up. "I'll go in partners with you in this home guard business, and we'll make it you and me against Lew and Charlie."

At that, Lew started to demur a bit. "It'll take a lot of money to go way up there," he said. "But make it two hundred, and I think we'll take you on."

"Fine!" exclaimed Birchy. "Well put up our hundred apiece right now. You fellows better get a hump on and pack your duffle. It'll be trapping time by the time you get a line staked out up there."

Maybe you think the rest of the boys didn't sit up and take notice at that? The air was charged with interest. Here was Lew and Charlie deciding right pronto to take the trip north they had been talking of and dreaming about for years, and here was Birchy and me, jumping into a two-hundred-dollar bet with them about who could rustle up the most fur.

Of course, they would have to subtract the expense of their trip north from their fur catch. It was going to be an exciting contest.

Lew and Charlie made a quick job of packing and left two days later for a little flag station on the railroad, up near the Canada line. They took a liberal assortment of traps, guns, and a lightweight camping outfit. From what we had heard of that country, it was pretty safe to figure on camping in some of the deserted lumber shacks that dot the brush-grown, cutover land.

Birchy and I also got busy. We were depending upon skill and cunning to win the bet. We would trap in thickly settled country, farming land with scattered groves of timber and some marshland that had been trapped ever since the first settlers pioneered over from New York State and Pennsylvania. We were up against two serious problems that trappers in settled country must always fight—thin fur and thick competition.

There had been a couple of cold spells with some light snow early in October, and we figured it would be the first week in November before the fur primed up. Our first task was to prospect our territory and lay out a plan of operation. Birchy decided to take on a marshy strip that lay south of us, perhaps five hundred acres, and specialize in mink and rats. The higher ground—sand and clay hills—fell to my lot. I had about three square miles that I figured I could work over without running up against much real competition.

We dug up all the traps we owned, borrowed a few more, and went over them carefully, putting them in first-class shape. We rigged up a couple of backpacks to carry traps and lunch. Birchy arranged to camp in a small river shack that belonged to some fishermen friends, and I elected to sleep at home. He took a 12 gauge for ducks and a .22 for the trapline. I carried my Game-Getter, and we both brought pocket axes and sharp knives.

Birchy left for his river camp Sunday evening, and I arranged to start to place my traps next morning. My first run lay down an old abandoned railroad grade. Both sides of the cut were honeycombed with dens, mostly woodchuck. Skunk was to be my mainstay; some possum, perhaps a couple of fox and a few coons, with a weasel later on, was about all I could hope for. I searched each den carefully and decided to set traps in the entrances of those that showed sign. Two looked particularly "skunky," so I built small brush pens over to the sides of the entrances to place traps there, also. This would avoid disturbing the rest of the animals who made that particular den their home. I baited the sets with dead sparrows.

The first day, I put 11 traps down that mile-long cut. It was still early morning, and I worked cautiously, not showing myself any more than I could help. I concealed each set carefully; I didn't want any traps lifted if I could avoid this trouble. From the cut, I jumped over into half a mile of beech and maple grove. I expected to land a few possum and perhaps a coon there. My traps were set about the entrances of tree dens.

Here I used rabbit meat for bait. A big gray fellow had jumped out of a corn shock right ahead of me, and after taking a dozen jumps, had made the mistake of stopping to look back at me. A charge of number sixes from the .410 barrel of my Game-Getter knocked him over at twenty-seven paces, and I cut him up in pieces for the freshest bait imaginable.

Leaving the grove, I skirted around a large eighty-acre field of corn and set traps in the dens I found along the brush-grown fence rows. I expected pretty fair luck from these sets.

From there, I went zigzagging back and forth to take in as much timber as I could. I knew most of the people living there. Most of them had willingly given me permission to trap their land when I had made a prospecting trip before. But when I came to an unfavorable prospect, I skipped the land and kept out of sight. It never pays to advertise that you are stringing out traps in settled country. I counted on losing some, but hopefully, this wouldn't come right at the start.

The country began to get rougher, and presently, I ran across fox sign. I don't pretend to be a professional fox catcher, but I have trapped a few and expect to catch a few more. I noted the places and resolved to bring along a couple of chickens for bait next morning. I always have my best luck placing fox traps among feathers.

Ahead of me lay a splendid trapping stream—a fine, large creek that wound among the clay hills—the only bit of water in my territory. But a string was tied to the fur lying along those banks. The stream was trapped by an old-timer named Wes Howell, and he just about believed he owned it, body and soul. If any trapper ventured in, he either bluffed 'em out or harassed 'em until they left. Old Wes could certainly pull off some tricks in trap stealing and fur pinching, and once in a while, a bullet whizzed over someone's head far too close for comfort. Nobody seemed to want to bother Wes any, and his reputation as a tough customer grew yearly.

But as I thought it over, I was just aching to set down along the banks of that stream. Wes never trapped it closely, and I knew I could pick up a dozen mink roaming along the water. Wes usually waited until rather late in the season, getting only the primest pelts and counting upon his strafing to protect the line until he was ready.

I stood and looked longingly down that river valley, figuring it might hold the key to winning our wager with Lew and Charlie. Presently, I heard footsteps behind me, and here came Wes himself. His keen old eye took in at a glance my pack sack of traps.

"Howdy," he said coldly. "Startin' a mite early, ain't you?"

"No, not for skunk," I answered. "Got to get them before the cold weather sets in and they hole up."

"Well," said he, "I figure on mostly mink this season, and I expect to wait a month more, and I ain't worryin' none but what they'll be there waiting for me," he added meaningfully. Then he turned back towards his cabin.

This remark made me mad, and I decided right then I was going into that valley in spite of Wes. He had no more right to the fur than I, and while I didn't like the sort of trouble he gave, I resolved to make a try. He had the advantage of living on the ground, and by having no scruples stooping to any trick—things a decent sportsman would never dream of doing. It wasn't any use to fight him openly, for all he had to do was to sneak about and watch for his chance of doing dirt. I decided to get a little sneaky, myself.

The morning after setting traps, I jumped out early and started my first check over the line. To say I was excited would be putting it mildly. A trapper always lives on hopes and dreams. Each day's earnings are uncertain. He may make a dollar and he may make fifty. Of course, he seldom does make that fifty, but this daydreaming of a lucky strike is what keeps him going over the rough patches and brings pleasure to an otherwise hard existence.

It had been a good night for fur to run, and I stepped briskly along, full of joyful anticipation. I knew if the first trap on the first morning held fur, my luck would be good, and a medium number one skunk sat bunched up before the first den, securely held in my double-jaw trap. The opposite bank yielded a number three skin, and I passed on to the beech grove. Here was a possum and one weasel. One trap had been sprung, and from the commotion, I judged a big coon had walked in and then right out of the light trap. I drew a No. 2 from my packsack and set it. Small steel hasn't much chance with big Northern coon.

My rabbit bait had drawn in another skunk, and I ended up, about the middle of the day, well pleased with the returns. No traps were missing, and no fur had been lifted. I knew, of course, my luck would change in this particular.

The next morning brought lighter returns—only a skunk, two weasels and a big coon, perhaps the one who had pulled out of my trap the night before. But he was a dandy and was going to help considerably in beating Lew and Charlie.

Birchy got me on the phone that night and said he had caught a few rats and a mink. Slow but steady. He had sixty traps out on the marsh and was having a hard time putting out more, for a lot of the best ground already was covered with traps. He was lying as low as he could.

The weather stayed cold but crisp, and I ran the line each morning for the next two weeks. The fur was light, but I pulled in a few skins. I averaged two skunks a day, until one Sunday morning when I skinned out four. That was a big day. I also got a nice red fox at a set baited with a piece of chicken. Another coon and two possum made for the biggest catch of my season that day.

That night, I decided to run down to the marsh and see how Birchy was coming. I hadn't heard from him in a week, and he had told me he was having a little trouble with two rascals who were trying to run him out. I jumped on a slow freight train at six o'clock, and an hour later dropped off beside the track and then tramped the two miles over to his shack.

A dim light burned in the window, and I stepped around to the door to walk inside. But just as I reached out for the latch, something warned me not to open that door. I had an uncanny feeling of evil. I am not easily scared or superstitious at all, but I just couldn't bring myself to grasp that door handle in the ominous calm that enveloped the mist-shaded marsh.

I backed quietly away and walked around to the single window at the back, took out my knife, worked about a pane until I could pry it loose from the putty. Pushing aside the curtain, I peered in.

The hair slowly arose on my head at what I saw in the dim light. There was Birchy's shotgun propped up before the door—with a string running from the door handle to the gun's trigger. Enough slack hung in the cord so the gun would be fired just as the door opened wide enough to admit a man. If I had jerked that door open, I would have received the load square in my body.

I didn't know where Birchy was or what had happened to him, but I suspected the devils who had rigged up that deadly trap were not far off. I stepped in through the window, opened the door, and discharged the gun. The roar echoed over the bog like a cannon. Then I lowered the light and waited.

Presently, the sound of running steps reached me. I straightened up alert, then settled down when I recognized Birchy's walk. He ran up and threw open the door. He held a short pistol in his hand—something I didn't know was in his outfit.

"What the heck …" he began, and then he saw me. "Where did you drop from, old-timer? Gosh, I'm glad to see you. It's been pretty tough sledding here the past three days."

There was no mistaking the welcome in his voice. I pulled him inside and in low tones told him what I had found awaiting behind the cabin door. His face paled in the dim light. "Those dirty …" he snapped. "Ain't that a sweet trick to play on a fellow man, just for the sake of a few rat and mink skins? And I've got as much right down here as any of them.

"Those two Lewellings are hounding me continually. I lost seven traps today," he went on soberly, "and I'm sure they rigged up that shotgun. Think they'll turn up to see how it worked?"

That was my exact idea. I whispered a minute to Birchy, and his face lit up. "Gosh, I'm glad you happened down tonight, old-timer. It'll take two of us, but we can handle those river rats."

We sat down quietly to await the men who set traps for other men. Perhaps we had baited and set a trap ourselves, and now were waiting to spring it.

We must have sat there in the dim lamplight an hour before a stealthy step outside the cabin roused us to tingling excitement. I nodded to Birchy, and he noiselessly laid himself out before the door on the floor, just where a man would have fallen after receiving a load of shot from the ambush gun.

I was stationed back out of sight of the rear window, my eyes fixed on the opening, waiting. Slowly, a ghostly hand appeared behind the curtain, pushed it back, and made just enough room for a swarthy, hair-covered face that peered over where Birchy lay outstretched on the rough floor.

I crouched back in my corner, every muscle taut. I hardly dared to breathe for fear of being heard. The head withdrew, and a low voice spoke. "We got 'im, Jule. He won't skin any more mink down here."

I was sore before, but nothing like the rage that filled me when I heard this callous remark. For all he knew, he had killed a fellow being, and his tone was devoid of sympathy or regret. Steps approached the door, and I gathered myself together. It swung open, and simultaneously, I launched myself at the foremost figure—just as Birchy reached out and tripped him by both ankles. This was my undoing. The man stumbled, and I lit sprawling on the floor behind. Before I could recover, another burly fellow in a mackinaw coat had a throttle hold on my neck, and I could tell it was not the first time he had choked another. He was an expert, alright. My ears rang, and black spots mingled with flashes of light before my eyes. I was weakening fast, and something had to be done. But I couldn't tear those hands from my throat. I remember as plain as print how his hot breath carried a horrible combination of stale tobacco and onions.

In a last attempt, I let go of those hands of steel, and pushing back his body to get some room, jerked my knee up into his stomach. I used all the strength I could gather. He grunted, and his grip relaxed a little. Again, I drove it into his belly, and again his grip loosened. Evidently, my blows nauseated him as I hoped. Then my hands tore his away.

Staggering back, I grabbed Birchy's shotgun and brought it down on his head just as he drew a long, evil-looking, hunting knife. He crumpled to the floor, and I turned in time to see Birchy finish the job of pounding his man into submission. With a final punch to the face, he arose, panting. "What now?" he gasped. "By rights, we ought to dump them in the river to drown."

"No, let's just pack up and clear out of here," I replied. "They are too thoroughly beaten up to damage us anymore, for a time. But I'm in favor of shaking the smell of this marsh off our clothes for good."

Birchy went over both men to see if they were armed. We didn't want to dump them outside and then have a stream of pistol bullets come back through the shack. He frisked a gun off of each and then hauled them out the door. The fellow I had slugged was starting to show signs of life, and we left them to make out as best they could.

After we heard them stumble away, we slept a bit, and then in the morning pulled up all of the traps Birchy had out and started home. He had a fairly good lot of fourteen mink and forty-six rats. Most of the mink were small, but they averaged up a neat sum. We both felt as though we had earned it all.

"I guess you saved my life, old timer," Birchy declared and then sat in sober silence. "I've no idea how many skins I lost besides the seven traps. It got so I had to run the line before daybreak to stay ahead of them."

Don't know why, but I happened to think of Lew and Charlie up north, laughed out loud, and said, "I guess Lew and Charlie picked the wrong end of this bet if they expected to get all of the excitement."

Then I told him about my plan to trap Wes Howell's "private" mink preserve.

"Sufferin' cats!" exclaimed Birchy. "Haven't we had enough excitement to last this season? The old cuss'll shoot you if you trap down there!"

"He won't get a look at me," I answered. "I'm going to work nights and early mornings. Believe me, we're going to clean up the fur and win that bet with Lew and Charlie!"

Next day, I packed a light shelter tent, my traps and some grub and set out. I arrived at the marsh in the middle of the night and dumped the duffle in a thicket, taking extra pains to hide all from sight. Then I set traps by torchlight until daylight, returned to the thicket, set up the tent, ate a little and turned in. I was dead tired and slept until late afternoon.

After dark, I started out again and placed the rest of the traps. Mink sign was thick, and a few rat tracks showed along the bank. I built a tiny fire, made a quart of hot tea, and spent a very comfortable night. I made nothing but drowning sets that would hide the catch underwater, and so far, I knew I had kept completely out of sight. But I also knew old Wes would be scouting about the valley every day.

Early the next morning, I ran the line for the first time in half-light. Two mink and one rat were my returns. I got back to camp undiscovered, and then began one of the longest days I've ever spent. I could only lay there restless and impatient, incapable of restful sleep.

Late in the day, I couldn't stand it any longer, got up and worked my way carefully to the mouth of the valley. Old Wes came strolling down the hillside, and I ducked just in time to escape being discovered. I lay in the brush, my heart in my mouth. One of my traps was set just ahead of him. I had made the mistake of coming up too far this way.

Then one of my lucky moments arrived. A red squirrel started to chatter up on the hill, and Wes stopped, listened a minute, and then turned and went back up the hill.

I scurried back to camp, carefully making my way through the thickest brush I could find. A few minutes later, I heard the sharp crack of a rifle and had no doubt that a red squirrel had saved me at the expense of its own life.

Next morning, I got but one mink and three rats. I carefully reset the traps and decided to go home for a break before returning to make a final trip over the line. I couldn't stand being cooped up in the tent for another day.

My two days' catch swelled our pile to respectable proportions. We began to wonder just how Lew and Charlie were making out. Nobody had heard a word from them, although that was not surprising.

I left that same night for a final run of my traps over at Wes Howell's. I got there well before sunrise and found the catch to be good. Four mink and two rats were drowned in the traps. I pulled each trap as fast as I came to it, and it was a good thing, because just as I reached the lower end of the valley I heard the crunch of boots on frosty ground, and here came old Wes with two of my traps in his hand and blood in his eye. If he had just looked around a bit he would have seen me, but he was too intent on finding more traps—the ones I had just pulled. I chuckled to myself all the way home.

We had a fine lot of mink, rats and skunk, with a few coon, possum, fox and weasel—an assortment to be proud of when one considered it was all gleaned from trapped-out country. We were pretty sure we would win the two-hundred-dollar bet, and we began to plan how we would spend it. We were considering new guns when a whistle sounded outside, and opening the door, we saw Bill, another member of our gang.

"Hurry!" he cried. "Lew and Charlie just got off of the noon train."

Of course, the bet was the uppermost thought in my mind, and I asked eagerly, "Did you see how much fur they brought?"

"You won, I guess," was the answer, "for all the fur they had was tied up in a little bundle Lew carried. I asked him if more stuff was coming by freight, but he shook his head. Can't be more than a half-dozen skins."

This is the story Lew and Charlie told us that night at the club shanty, of their adventures up in the Northern bush country—a tale about which we all talked and wondered for many months. I have written down exactly as they told it to us that night.

Chapter 2 – Lew & Charlie in the Northwoods

The boys stepped off from the train, nearly a week after their departure from home. It was the end of the branch line—a warped, wavy stretch of rusting rails and rotting ties. Endless acres of cutover, decaying stumps and brush stretched out in all directions. The railroad had followed a low, marshy valley the last fifteen miles, through which straggled several streams—ideal trapping ground. Back on either side, just where the eye lost its sharp definition, the ground began to rise, low hills that mounted and grew until, right at the hazy margin that marked the limits of sight, they merged into bluffs, a range of hills or knobs that fairly smelled of marten.

They looked at each other and grinned approvingly. "I guess we've hit the right spot, partner," said Lew.

They gathered their baggage and looked around. Neither had much idea about where or which way to go; they merely wanted to be gone out towards the hills and into the stretches of birch and spruce.

There was but one building besides the station, a rambling one-story structure built of sawmill slabs and bearing a sign identifying it as post office and general store. On a bench before the door sat half a dozen Native Cree with swarthy faces and straight black hair, clad in broad-checked shirts and overalls. Charlie paused before them, stretched an arm towards upriver, and said, "We want to hire a boat to haul us out of here, up towards those hills."

For a while no one spoke. The men looked at each other, then back at Charlie. Finally, a squat barrel of a man said, "Poitre got a boat."

A Cree sitting at the end of the bench half rose, thereby admitting his identity. He spoke slowly. "River swift. You pole. Two dollar."

This offer was promptly accepted. Turning next into the store, they bargained for a month's supply of grub: flour, beans, bacon, rice and prunes. Wallet in hand, Charlie stood waiting for the bill when the door opened and a woman staggered in.

The storekeeper looked up from his figures in irritation. "Now you get out of here, Sally Long-Bear. I've got nothing for you. You're drunk!"

She steadied herself against the jamb. "I no drink, I starve!" She swayed as she spoke. Lew and Charlie looked questioningly at the man.

"Ever since her man died last summer, she don't do nothing but hang around the store and beg," he explained. "I staked her for a while, but I can't afford to keep it up forever. Why don't she go back to her folks over on Sissinong Creek? They'd take her in."

And then he bent back over his figures.

The woman was plainly about gone. Obeying a strong impulse, Charlie stepped over and pressed a bill into her hand.

"This will spell you awhile," he said kindly.

She looked up in surprise, as much from the kindness in his voice as the size of the gift. Then she drew herself up with an effort and spoke rapidly in Cree. Charlie smiled and walked back to pay for their grub. Still grumbling, the storekeeper helped them pack the food up in duffle bags.

When they reached the river, Poitre silently indicated his boat, a wide, flat-bottomed dugout chained to the bank. Lew and Charlie walked down with their food, boxes of traps and camp equipment. The dugout had been laboriously hewn from a single monstrous log. The sides were straight and true and hardly thicker than bark. Inside, a marvelous frame of pliant spruce gave it the rigidity and strength of a craft built of lumber. In addition, it was nearly as light as a canvas or bark canoe.

"Wasn't that a fair-sized bill you gave away in the store?" asked Lew. "Will we have to count that as expenses in our wager with Birchy and Slim?"

"It was bigger than I realized, at first, but I couldn't stand the look of suffering in her eyes. It's my own money, too, and need not be counted in with the cost of our trip."

Soon, Poitre strode down the bank, threw in a sack of supplies of his own, and loosened the boat. Handing a pole to each of them, he pointed upstream. They poled steadily until noon, when a short stop was made. Poitre brewed a can of tea and lunched silently from a bag of store crackers. The trappers made coffee and fried bacon. The stream began to get swifter late in the afternoon. It was nearly dusk when Poitre pointed to a long, V-shaped ripple cut cleanly from the nose of a swimming animal.

"Otter," he said.

Lew and Charlie thrilled at the sight. They were sure this country was right for them. Poitre beached the boat and pointed up a tiny brush-grown stream that forked off away from the hills that loomed in the half-light.

"Live there," he said, pointing. "Hills there," he added, indicating a different direction, and then he waited for them to unload. Poitre received their money in silence and then poled swiftly for home.

Plans were made that night around the campfire. It was agreed to backpack the outfit in up near the edge of the hills, where they would be close to upland and lowland trapping. By loading themselves heavily, they could make it in two trips and figured it would take a day or two.

They started the next morning before the sun was fully up, following a route along the smaller stream, and when they had tramped about ten miles, they stumbled into a rough log camp that sat squarely up against a steep hill. It looked clean, although in rather bad repair.

They stopped up a den in the dirt floor that looked very much as though a clever skunk had decided to take advantage of man's enterprise. Soon, a fire blazed in the clay fire-hole that utilized a tunnel worked up through the cliff at the rear of the shack for a chimney; beds of spruce were gathered and thatched upon the floor.

The following morning was spent bringing up the balance of the supplies. Then both started out in opposite directions to prospect for fur and lay out probable lines for the next morning.

Night brought back two tired and badly discouraged fur prospectors. They looked ruefully at each other across the split puncheon table. Not an acre of fur country had either found that was not already posted and being trapped. Native trappers were camped within six miles of the cabin.

"We'll try it again tomorrow, old man," said Charlie. "Then, if we don't find room for our traps, we'll have to move on, farther into the hills."

Charlie was home first that evening. Just before he reached the cabin, a pair of grouse flew up from right under his feet and then foolishly perched on the low branch of a spruce fifty yards away. He stalked carefully to easy range for his belt pistol and bagged both, the first through the head and the second with a speedy body shot before the bird gathered headway leaving the tree.

As he turned back to the cabin clearing he stopped. A boat was beached on the stream bank. "We must have visitors," he thought, and then walked warily to the door.

Before the fire sat the Cree woman whom he had given money to back at the store. She stood up and burst into a rapid flow of Cree, punctuated by vigorous gesticulations. Then, evidently remembering he could not understand, she stopped, smiled faintly, and continued in broken English.

"Sally Long Bear," she began. "You come trap? Yes? No find fur here, all gone. My people thick—traps here, there, all places. You gave me money— save my life, maybe. Come with me. My man's trapline empty, but plenty mink, marten, otter, fox."

She waved her arms to express the magnitude of the territory and the abundance of fur, and Charlie's heart leaped as he realized the opportunity she offered them.

"Where is this trapline?" he asked. But before she could answer, Lew entered the cabin, and when Charlie quickly filled him in, his face also lit up with hope.

The woman made them understand the territory of her departed husband lay about eighteen miles north, could be reached by water in one day's travel, and there were cabins to use for camps.

The woman assured them she held all rights, and the other Cree respected her claim. She would expect a few furs in return, enough to ensure her tea, flour, and a few staples for the winter.

The woman's boat was big enough to carry them and their outfit. She had laboriously poled upstream for two days to find them and extend this offer. They decided to waste no time and start out early the next morning.

They poled back downstream for perhaps two hours. Then the woman signaled them to pole over to the bank. Nearing thick brush, they could feel an incoming current pushing at the boat. Sally directed them to push right into the tangled growth as she sat in the bow, skillfully pushing and pulling the boat until a hidden waterway became more open, and then they emerged into a sluggish creek the casual voyageur would never have guessed existed.

By noon, they were poling up through a wide, marshy lake. The woman steered straight across and then ran the boat up on shore. "Portage," she said, and then pointed towards a low ridge a few yards off. Lew and Charlie looked at the load and then at the boat doubtfully. The boat alone weighed an easy two hundred pounds, and if the distance was of any length …

But the woman waved them on impatiently. They unloaded, took either end of the boat, and staggered up the ridge. At the top, both whistled in surprise. There, almost at their feet, lay a tiny lake, and from one end a bigger stream flowed away.

"It's a natural divide!" cried Lew. "That river runs exactly opposite from the one we came up on."

Renewed by this unexpected development, they were reloaded and off in a matter of minutes. The new river was swift, and they made fast time down its course. The day turned sharp and cold, and before night, a thin skim of ice crackled before the prow of the boat as it passed through deep, quiet pools.

Charlie knew what this meant. It foretold the long winter that would soon sweep down from the North, an icy shroud of chill and blasting cold. What water trapping they might do must be started at once.

Dark found them comfortably ensconced in the main cabin of the departed Native trapper whose line they were about to set.

In the morning, Sally sketched upon the ground with a birch twig a map of the trapping grounds. It lay along both banks of the river, bounded upon one side by a steep ridge of hills and upon the other by a deep morass of undergrowth, mostly birch—a white belt that could not be mistaken. She filled in her crude map marking the fallen logs to be used as footbridges, and then the best set locations for marten on the ridge; otter, mink and fisher along the river; fox and weasel in the birch. Then she drew in the other rough cabins for overnight camps—one up on the ridge and others over near the marsh. At the farthest boundary by the river, she indicated another cabin but then spoke sternly in mixed Cree and English.

"No go, no go," she repeated, over and over. "Death," she declared, followed by a swift flow of guttural Cree. She would not stop until both Lew and Charlie had promised to stay away from the place. But each also registered in his mind a resolve to learn more about it, when opportunity presented itself.

Then followed a busy and joyful week. It was wonderful sport to string out loops of traps, following faint blaze marks on the trees that still were visible. They put out a loop each day, also running the first sets that needed tending, and the fur began to accumulate. Nothing heavy, but fine pelts, mostly mink and rats, now and then a marten, and once an otter. Lew shot his first deer, a splendid buck that jumped from cover within a quarter-mile of camp. Venison hung in the cabin that night, and both felt they were living the free and splendid life of a Northern trapper. Charlie packed a quarter of the deer down to where the Cree woman preferred to live alone in a smaller cabin.

The weather grew steadily colder. Water sets had to be made only in fairly swift current or they would freeze fast. Finally came the day when all traps were out, and both men left early in the morning to run the lines. It was both a lucky and an ominous day. It brought them the best catch of the season: a deep-furred otter, three rats, a fox, some weasels, a mink and a marten. It also ushered in the arrival of Blackhawk and his murderous band.

It had been a hard day's tramp, but when Lew and Charlie met in the woods on their way in, both were jubilant over the catch. That changed when they reached the cabin and found three strangers squatting before the door and the Cree woman standing in the opening. She was speaking loud and fast, and her eyes snapped with anger as she berated one of the men who sat in stoic silence. He was a tall, full-blooded Cree. The other two were more poorly dressed half-breeds, men with shifty eyes and ugly faces.

"What's the matter?" asked Charlie.

"I am Blackhawk," the obvious leader spoke, "brother of Long-Bear. His trapline now mine, next blood." Then he pointed to the woman, "She had no right to sell to you."

Then he grinned complacently and said, "You move on, now."

Lew and Charlie looked at each other doubtfully. The woman burst in before either could reply. "He lie!" she cried. "Trapline mine!"

The Cree merely bowed at that and then smoothly straightened to his full imposing height. No doubt he was a powerful man, lithe and agile as a panther.

"Line mine," he said. Then he pointed at their catch. "Fur mine, too, leave it. No want trouble, but I take."

Then he started off into the timber, whistled once, and the other two rose and swiftly followed. Both Lew and Charlie noted the surprising silence of their stealthy strides.

Here was a real complication, just when things were running smoothly and the fur was coming in regularly. At the rate they were going, they would have easily cinched the wager of two hundred dollars they had made back at the Club House.

"Blackhawk liar, thief!" the woman spat out. "You go on trap!" Then she paused as if suddenly remembering some vital point forgotten in her anger. "Blackhawk bad," she added slowly. "Kill man in Montreal."

The trappers discussed the situation far into the night.

"One thing," said Lew. "We don't just pull out. Let's keep trapping and see what they do. We'll grab all the fur we can; we'll have a splendid catch in a week. Do you think they'll make trouble right away?"

That was a hard one for Charlie to answer. Blackhawk might be a braggart, a boaster who made idle threats. On the other hand, the sinister cast of his and his companions' faces might accurately bespeak character. He could not forget the silent, stealthy tread—a gait that somehow bespoke crafty cunning. Blackhawk, he surmised, would make a dangerous enemy.

The morning sun arose upon a world of white. Heavy, thick snow enveloped everything. Nothing remained undraped to break the colorless expanse. Charlie opened the door and started for the river for a pail of water. "Why, what's this?" he said.

Lew stepped out beside him. There before the threshold lay a snowshoe rabbit with an arrow through its body. The rabbit lay on its side, with the arrow point protruding several inches.

"Looks like a weather vane," Lew replied dryly.

"I believe you are nearer right than you suspect," answered Charlie thoughtfully. "Somebody laid that dead rabbit here for a purpose. See? The arrow points due south."

Lew picked it up. "Why, one leg has been cut off; it only has three feet left. I'm sure it means something. And I'm afraid it won't be good news, either. I will go down and see if the woman can read the sign."

Sally Long-Bear muttered to herself when she saw the rabbit. "Blackhawk's sign," she said. "You must leave, go where arrow points. Three feet means you have three days."

She looked frightened.

Lew and Charlie ate a hasty breakfast and then started out to check traps. Evidently, the heavy snow had discouraged fur from running, for neither collected a single hide. Each trap was empty and untouched.

After they returned and were sitting at the table, Lew said, "It's funny not to find even a sprung trap. We had such good luck before. Why, there wasn't even a porcupine moving today."

As soon as Charlie arose the next morning he made straight for the door. He had the manner of one who is looking for something and yet dreads to find it. He was not disappointed. Another rabbit lay transfixed with an arrow. The arrow pointed south, and there were only two feet on this body.

That day proved the same as the one before. Not a trap held fur. Toward the end of his line, Charlie began to get suspicious. It was snowing lightly yet steadily enough to cover his tracks of the day before, yet several times he found places where the snow seemed more packed than it should have been, as though feet had pressed down before the prints were covered again with fresh snow, and some of these places he knew he had not walked.

He was on the marten ridge, where the sets were mostly in trees, when a bit of torn bark caught his eye. It was below a trap he had not touched since setting. Someone or something had climbed that tree. He looked at it closely; then he started digging carefully at the base. His suspicions were verified when he uncovered bloodstained snow. Someone had taken an animal from the trap and then tried to conceal the evidence. Instantly, the whole thing flashed upon him. Blackhawk and his men were running their lines every morning ahead of them, gathering the fur and resetting the traps.

He hurried home at his best speed. Something must be done to meet this direct challenge. Lew met him at the cabin, and his face fell when he saw his partner also empty-handed. "Not a hair in any of my traps today," he said. "I was sure you'd have a little luck."

Charlie immediately told him of his discovery.

"Of course!" cried Lew. "I saw several things that should have alerted me, but I was too disappointed to see the real meaning. What shall we do?"

"If I knew what they were planning when our three days are up, I'd feel better," Charlie began. "They may be running a bluff to scare us out, and, then again, they may be truly dangerous. We're in strange country. They are at home, and they've got the advantage in every way. Looks like we might as well pull out before things get any worse."

The unknown always worries us most. Something bad but tangible loses the terror of uncertainty. The trappers decided to make an extra early start the next morning. Perhaps they could catch Blackhawk and his men stealing their fur, and then they could have it out with them.

The third rabbit was before the door when Lew opened it that morning. The arrow still pointed south, and three feet were missing. Only one day left. If the next rabbit had all four feet missing, what would happen that day?

Charlie made a quick trip around his line. It was only necessary to glance at each set as he passed. All were empty as before. He reached home first and was starting a fire when Lew burst in, shaking with excitement.

"I caught one today," he cried. "One of those crooks was stooping over my trap, taking out a mink. I knocked him down, and when he came back at me with a knife, I shot him in the shoulder. He slumped down and whimpered then walked away cursing me."

Then he continued much more soberly, "Charlie, that's the first time I ever pointed a gun at a man, and I had to shoot him."

"I'm sorry that happened, Lew, although I know I'd have done the same," Charlie assured him. "I think we had better pull out now, while we can get away without losing anything more. If you had met up with Blackhawk himself, I doubt you would have gotten off so easily."

Charlie decided to post a watch that night. He was afraid of a surprise attack; their enemies were as stealthy as lynx, and they could not risk being at such a disadvantage. Lew agreed to take the first guard. It was ghostly still; nothing broke the silence of the Northern night except the snapping of frost. Once he thought he heard a faint rustle outside a wall, crept over and peered out through a chink but could see nothing. He dared not unbar and open the door.

Charlie took his place at midnight. A rabbit screamed out in the timber. He could not suppress a shudder at the sound. Perhaps that same rabbit would lie before their door in the morning.

At daybreak he unfastened and opened the door. Then he called Lew. Both paled as they looked. There was no arrow this time. The rabbit had been disemboweled, and all four legs had been severed. They needed no interpreter to read the threat conveyed.

Charlie stepped back into the cabin, every nerve alert and tingling. Danger was a stimulant to him; proximity to peril turned him into a dynamo of resolve. "Come, hustle, Lew! We must pack up and be out of here in half an hour."

It was then Lew displayed the stubborn streak that was to cost them dearly. He refused point-blank to budge until they gathered in all of their traps. He insisted they must then move farther into the hills, to prospect another line and go home with enough fur to win their wager.

In vain, Charlie argued the danger of delay. Lew insisted they were a match for Blackhawk and his men, because one was already wounded, the one he had shot in the shoulder. Charlie was older and better versed in the ways of evil men. He knew the attack would not come in the open, but it would be nonetheless deadly, sly and stealthy.

However, seeing it was useless to waste further time in talk, he agreed to round up the traps they could carry in one quick trip and leave those staked the farthest away. He expected to load their belongings in the boat belonging to the Cree woman, and keeping to the open center of the stream, follow it as far as they could. Sooner or later, he was sure it must reach a settlement, perhaps a post of considerable size. And they stood a fair chance of locating other trapping ground after that.

They left the cabin on the double quick. Pushing hard, they expected to be in with a load of traps shortly after noon. But it was hard going. The snow had piled up during three days' fall, and the trails were level full. Both kept a sharp look about for danger or an ambush. Charlie hated to leave the cabin and venture out separately, but as long as Lew could not be convinced of the danger, he felt a quick start would save the most time.

Nothing happened on the trail, and the traps were empty as before. Charlie returned heavily loaded with steel and found his partner standing a hundred yards from the cabin, watching it warily.

"Anything wrong?" he asked.

Lew motioned him closer. "I haven't heard anything, but it looks from here as if a fresh trail leads up to the door, tracks we didn't make."

"Well, let's get it over with," said Charlie, and he started towards the door. "Come on!"

Fifty yards was as close as they got. A rifle cracked, and a bullet, striking at their feet, puffed a cloud of snow into their faces. They froze in their tracks. The shot had been fired from the cabin.

Charlie hailed loudly. "Who's there, and what do you want?"

No sound broke the silence. He advanced a step farther, and a second bullet whistled past his face before he heard the crack of gunfire, this one so close his skin tingled with the sting of speeding metal. He fell back instinctively.

"Whew!" he gasped. "They mean business. That's as close as I ever want to get to a high-power bullet."

Still no sound or movement from the cabin. The ghostly silence increased the sense of danger. They turned back and regrouped in the timber.

"Looks like we must camp in the brush tonight," said Charlie. "They intend to hold the fort, and from the way they shoot, I see no point in contesting that fact."

He dropped the sacks of traps. "No use lugging these any farther, either," he said.

Lew flushed a little at that and then said haltingly, "I'm sorry I was bull-headed. You were right. By now we should be twenty miles downriver. It looks as if we'll be lucky to pull through this with our lives."

"Oh, we'll pull through, all right," said Charlie calmly. "They had plenty of chance to shoot us, so I know they fear the law and won't kill us in cold blood. They have something else up their sleeves, I'm sure. But we've got our guns, and we'll manage somehow."

They started off deeper into the timber. "We'll make a shelter out here," Charlie began, "and then in the morning we'll go over and see if the Cree woman can stake us a blanket or two. We'll borrow her boat and beat it downstream. We can shoot enough game to carry us through, and it won't be two weeks before we'll be back in the club shanty telling the home guys some real adventures." Then Charlie laughed encouragingly.

They tramped for an hour and finally chose a thick grove of young spruce. Charlie had a belt ax, and they both carried knives. They used these to make a rough lean-to, covering the poles with spruce boughs, and then they thatched a thick bed underneath. They brought in firewood until the pile looked big enough to last through two nights. Without blankets, the fire had to burn steadily.

"It takes a terrible lot of wood to last a cold Northern night," said Charlie. "The only safe way is to get twice as much as you think you'll need, and even then sometimes you run short."

The fire blazed before the rough spruce shelter, and sitting back on the fragrant evergreens, they were fairly comfortable except for a weakening feeling at the belt line. Neither had eaten since morning. Lew grinned ruefully as he thought of the big pan of prunes he had put to soaking in anticipation of a final camp feast on their return.

"We must catch a rabbit for breakfast," he said. "Have we anything to make a snare? Tomorrow we will surely shoot meat of some sort. We've been giving the Cree woman a share whenever we shot game, but she hasn't anymore than enough to see herself through."

A search of pockets disclosed a spare leather shoelace. Lew took it, and lighting his way with a torch of rich heartwood, looked for a rabbit trail. Finally, he located a fairly fresh run and propped an open noose across it.

When he got back to camp, they discussed the necessity of standing guard. "I don't think we will be attacked in camp, at least not early. They know we have guns, and they already have something thought up, the way they act. Let's put on just enough wood to last until midnight and sleep. When the cold wakes us, from then on we'll take turns watching."

Both were warmly clad, and the spruce shelter broke the wind. They curled up and slept for perhaps three hours before waking up shivering. They piled on more wood, and as soon as the heat renewed symptoms of drowsiness, Charlie moved back from the blaze and bade Lew sleep.

For hours, it seemed, Charlie sat beside the fire, his rifle across his knee. His mind was puzzling over what Blackhawk and his band had in store. They already had captured the cabin and the fur. What more would they do to them? Charlie knew the threat in the disemboweled rabbit had been direct. Real danger lay ahead, unseen and unknown.

Then a faint slush, slush, like snowshoes pushing soft snow, aroused him with a start. He rolled swiftly back from the circle of firelight and lay tense in the shadows. He called to Lew in a loud whisper, "Wake up! They're coming!"

Lew slept on like a log. In desperation, Charlie picked up a short piece of wood and threw it at him. The slush, slush came nearer. Lew turned over and muttered in his sleep. Charlie renewed his low calls, and finally his partner sat up. "What the …" he began, and then his keen ear caught the sound, and he scrambled back from the fire and lay beside Charlie.

"What is it?" he whispered. Charlie shook his head and strained his eyes on the ghostly shadows. A faint wind moaned through the trees overhead. The snow-covered timber took on spectral shapes. Away back in the hills a wolf howled, a drawn-out wail that raised the hairs along their spines.

A dark object, low to the ground, ambled into view.

"Is it a man creeping on his hands?" whispered Charlie, pointing his rifle.

Lew broke out in a chuckle. "No, it's just breakfast—coming in under its own power."

Then he stood up, and seizing a stout limb from the pile of wood, stepped over and whacked a big porcupine over the head. "I won't object to porky when I'm half-starved," he said with another chuckle.

Charlie curled up on the browse and was soon asleep. Lew stretched his cramped muscles and prepared to stand watch.

To this day, Lew doesn't remember if he fell asleep or not. He has dim memories or colorless visions, perhaps a dream of stealthy footsteps and a touch upon his shoulder. His head was light from want of food and the cold, and it is hard to say which part of the chimera that troubles his mind really happened. But he found himself erect with the camp ax raised in one hand, shouting for his partner to awaken.

Charlie tumbled out of the shelter and ran to him. Lew pointed dazedly to a trail of moccasin tracks vanishing off into the forest. "Our guns!" he cried.

Charlie looked swiftly about. Both rifles were gone. "Why didn't you wake me? What were you doing?" The questions poured forth like gunshots.

Lew sank on the snow and groaned. "I … I don't know, Charlie. I must have slept. No, I couldn't have been really asleep. I must have just dozed. I heard a twig snap and then saw two figures running off among the trees, carrying our rifles in their hands."

Charlie snatched the pistol from his belt and started down the trail, but a dozen steps brought him to his senses. He turned and walked slowly back to the fire. Lew was sitting with a look of dejection on his face. The first pale light of a new day brought him no solace.

"Never mind, old boy," said Charlie softly. "Let's skin the porky and eat. Even porcupine meat will put some life into us. Maybe you have a rabbit in the snare? Run and see. I'll tackle the quill hog. Take my pistol."

Lew came back with a half-grown rabbit in hand. "Here's dessert," he called, the prospect of food bringing back his spirits, as always.

They ate heartily. The porky meat was strong and tough from lack of parboiling, but hungry men are not picky. The average city man, traveling in heated cars and living in an apartment with summer-like temperatures, is badly put out missing a meal during winter. Now, think of Lew and Charlie, tramping and sleeping in zero cold, sitting in the snow devouring half-cooked porcupine hams, their first meal in more than a day. No doubt, the Northern trapper feels the lack of food twice as hard.

Porcupines have been the salvation of many a trapper lost without a firearm in the woods. They are about the only meat one can catch by hand, kill with a club, and roast over a campfire. That has saved many a life. But charred, half-raw meat is no treat.

Charlie dressed the rabbit but left on the skin.

"We'll save it for tonight," he said.

The hot food brought back their strength, and they considered their situation. Charlie's pistol held but seven cartridges, of small caliber, and he decided to keep them in reserve as long as possible. They would serve better for hunting than battle. They decided to visit the cabin of the Cree woman who had brought them to her late husband's trapline and barter for her boat. Charlie slung the rabbit over his shoulder, and they struck out.

They strode briskly along, backtracking their trail made the night before. Both kept a close watch for any sign of danger and halted quickly when a black shadow became visible beside a spruce in the trail ahead. It strongly resembled a man hiding in ambush. They stopped just in time.

A rifle shot rang through the air, and a bullet plowed at their feet.

"Evidently, this way is closed," said Charlie. "Let's try a detour."

He was secretly worried by a thought that persisted in the back of his brain. They struck off to the left, and Charlie resolved to put this idea to a test. He turned back toward the north, and another bullet plunked before them, heading them off from this direction, too. They turned to the left, tried again, and were again halted by a shot.

"I thought so," said Charlie grimly. "They intend to force us back, either downriver or over into that swamp to lose ourselves and starve or freeze. That's why they have been so careful not to hit us with any of those shots. They are planning to let the cold kill us, so they cannot be convicted of our murders."

They tramped steadily for several hours. "Let's see if they are still dogging our steps," said Lew, and they turned off to one side and began to skirt back around their trail. They had not taken more than fifty steps before the rifle cracked. No doubt, they were being shadowed by a determined and alert enemy. The intent of the marksman had assumed inescapable meaning. They smiled grimly at each other, yet there was no use losing strength worrying about what they could not confront. Still, Charlie thought to himself, "If we only had our rifles …"

They were approaching the final lower loop of their trapline, where a number of sets still remained. They decided to check, since one might have caught a rabbit, which would certainly be more welcome than any fur pelt at this point. And Charlie also decided to pick up a couple of the smaller traps to set each night in rabbit paths.

Their luck was good. A big rabbit was frozen in one trap. Over behind a hill, some distance from their path, was a fox set, and Lew climbed down the slope to check it. Presently, Charlie heard him shout, and then he appeared waving something over his head.

"Can we eat it?" asked Charlie.

"No, but we can't go home without it," said Lew. "And I'll be glad to carry this one pelt whether our trail is a hundred or five hundred miles long."

"If we don't starve or freeze first," muttered Charlie under his breath, but he said nothing to dampen Lew's newfound enthusiasm.

It was a terribly long day. Toward the end, both began to suffer severely from cold and hunger. Thirst also bothered them not a little. The melted snow in Lew's canteen was gone, and they were wise enough not to eat snow. Charlie advised an early camp so more could be melted beside the fire—a slow process, but the only way. They had been forced away from the river by a series of steep, rough bluffs, and they could not tell when they would gain its bank again.

That night they repeatedly awoke half-frozen, and as soon as the fire brought comfort, the pangs of hunger gnawed within. The rabbits had made two fair meals, but they craved hot drink or soup, something to allay the bitter wind which froze the very marrow in their bones.

In the morning they resumed their march, stumbling along, tripping and falling over rocks and brush, breaking into brief runs over any clear going. Lew was beginning to give out under the strain. At noon he insisted upon lying down to rest. Charlie built a small fire, melted more snow and refilled the canteen, and then he dragged Lew back up to his feet to continue.

Both caught sight of the cabin simultaneously. They cried out in relief at the sight of the rough, split-log shack. "We'll sleep warm tonight," cried Lew, his strength coming back with a rush as he started on a trot for the building. But fate decreed differently. Even as he ran, the door slowly opened an inch, two—and then a rifle barrel thrust slowly toward them.

There was no need to fire the warning shot to ward them off. They turned and tramped wearily past the cabin. Their foes were determined to give them no comfort whatsoever. This came about as near to breaking their spirits as anything. The moment of anticipating a warm fire and bed had been brief but intense. "Another night in the snow," Lew groaned.

As they passed the cabin, Charlie looked back and saw a crude cross sticking up through the snow. He gave it but a brief thought. Then that night, as they sat in a lean-to before the fire, supperless and giddy from lack of food, he remembered what Sally had said about avoiding a place of death.

He sat up suddenly and said, "That was the cabin Long-Bear's widow warned us about, the place of death! Why, her man must have died there. Remember she also said something about the spotted sickness? Smallpox! That was Long-Bear's grave outside."

"And Blackhawk and his men were in there!" exclaimed Lew. "Lordy, wasn't it lucky they beat us to it? Why, we'd have taken the smallpox sure!"

And then he jumped up and fairly danced. "They'll catch it, sicken and die," he said. "We're avenged, even if we freeze and die out here in the woods."

Then he sank down, weakened by the sudden excitement. "It's poor consolation, though. Wonder what Birchy and Slim are doing back home? Suppose they are thinking of us?"

"Listen, somebody is coming!" whispered Charlie. He drew the pistol and looked out into the shadows. Lew listlessly followed his gaze. "It don't make much difference what they do, now," he said. "I'm about all gone."

A form approached, and Charlie lifted the pistol.

"No shoot!" a voice cried. "Me friend!"

"It's Long-Bear's widow," gasped Lew.

He jumped up and ran to meet her, and she handed him a copper kettle heavily loaded. "Hooray!" he yelled. "It's meat, and blessed if she hasn't brought tea, too!"

Charlie claims Lew kissed the woman in his joy, though Lew denies this. He does admit he danced about the fire before finally falling down in the snow from weakness. Charlie threw more wood on the fire, and the woman deftly hung the kettle over the blaze, put in some snow, and soon the appetizing aroma of stewed meat filled the air.

It seemed hours before the food was cooked. Then the Cree woman handed each a tin cup and sat smiling faintly as they plunged into the steaming kettle. They ate until caution warned against over-indulgence. Then, remembering her kindness, they turned sheepishly and thanked her.

"No, no," she replied. "You save me, I save you. We even now."

And she smiled with satisfaction. "We go, boat on river, come!"

Under her direction, they heaped up the spruce to resemble two covered, sleeping forms and piled the fire high with wood. This would deceive Blackhawk's gang should any of them leave the cabin to spy upon their camp in the night.

Her boat was tied to a fallen log that reached out past the frozen margin into the stream's moving current. They climbed in, released the rope, and the boat shot downriver.

It was a wild ride. Skillful poling was necessary to dodge the ice and brush that margined each sharp curve in the course. Twice they crashed into sunken logs, invisible in the soft shadows of the moon, jolts that strained the seams of the craft and sent tiny sprays of water shooting through.

In the small hours of the next morning, they were far enough away to be safe from pursuit, and they landed to make tea. After a short rest, the journey was resumed, and at noon, the final stop was made.

The Cree woman pointed. "Ten miles up valley, white man camp."

They thanked her with fervor. Charlie offered her more money, but she shook her head.

"Blackhawk die," she said. "Then fur he stole from you all mine."

She handed them the copper kettle and the tea, turned her boat about, and without another word, poled deftly against the current until she disappeared from sight. As they stood watching her from the bank, Lew finally spoke.

"That money you handed her in the store was your best investment ever. Come on, let's hurry. We can make ten miles by noon."

*   *   *

Back at the Rat Lake Club House, when the story had been told, we all sat back and looked at each other. Then Birchy jumped up and said, "I declare Lew and Charlie won the bet! If they had brought back what was caught the first week, we'd have lost. I say let's hand over the two hundred dollars!"

A burst of applause greeted this generous offer.

"Hold on a minute," said Lew. "We're not asking for charity. You haven't seen the fur we did bring back. Hand the bundle over, Charlie."

He took the long, thin package and undid the wrapping. Then he shook out before our astonished eyes the most magnificent silvery black pelt any of us had ever seen.

"A silver fox!" gasped Birchy. "Gosh, that beats us twice over!"

(The end)

The Fur Pocket on Big Thunder
Chapter 1 – The Man with the Yellow Teeth

Big Thunder flows irregularly, like a silver thread spun between the timbered knobs of the Cold Water Range, looping lazily through long, winding, mountain valleys and then tumbling over limestone shoals, plunging among glacial boulders that have been ground smooth and round by ages of rushing water until they lay like giant buckshot upon the river bed.

The Big Thunder country lies back among the hills and peaks, safe from the intrusion of tourists. Two twisting trails lead back into this vastness, but they are mere saddle paths, full of danger and difficult for any motor vehicle to traverse. A few battered flivvers wheeze and groan over these rough paths, but they are manned by intrepid drivers who fear neither man nor nature.

Only a thin sprinkling of rugged pioneers and mountain men inhabit the draws and valleys of Big Thunder, and they make little contact with the outside world. A star rider swims the fords twice a week with a meager bag of mail, and periodic trips are made down to the nearest settlement for such supplies as the hardy woodsmen cannot wring and squeeze from the timber, soil and water that hem in their hewed-log cabins. Such wants are few.

Sometimes, an adventurous hunter or trapper pushes back into the hills, braving the rough trails and cold suspicion of the mountain folk. Usually, these men leave after a few weeks, although one more hardy, more tenacious and contriving than the rest will entrench on some windswept hillside and become a settler, himself.

Such a man was Dale Harmon. And many miles lay between the tiny homestead that sheltered Dale and his daughter Anne and the home of Charlie and Lew, who, since their near-deadly expedition after fur in the Northern bush country, had felt but resisted the steady call of new country, where trails are fresh and adventure beckons from mountain and plain, from lake and stream.

But fate smiles at mere distance, and the intervening miles were swept away as a prairie fire sweeps the cured buffalo grass from the plains. The links in this chain of life were forged from stolen jewels, an old man's body shattered by bullets from a bandit's pistol, a helpless girl in a lonely cabin besieged by designing men, and a strip of virgin trapping ground rich in the furs of our Southern mountains. All came together to bridge the gap of distance and gather the principal actors in the most vivid drama of all—life—to act their parts and speak their lines.

*   *   *

Lew whistled softly to himself as he walked home from the club shack on Rat Lake where a group of hunters and trappers gathered each week to swap yarns, to tell of past exploits and plan others for the future. It was later than usual, after midnight, and he strode rapidly through the dark streets towards his father's house at the opposite end of town.

He was hoping his father would not be waiting for him. He did not approve of his son's company down at the lake, and had predicted countless times that trouble would result.

As Lew passed Shand's Jewelry Shop he glanced casually in through the darkened windows. Then he stopped abruptly as a thin light flashed in the rear of the store before fading so quickly he stood wondering if he had really seen it at all, or if his eyes had tricked his brain. He approached the glass and pressed his face against it. Everything was still and dark inside.

Lew started on his way but then paused again. Obeying some impulse that seized his mind and directed his steps, he stole noiselessly to the rear of the store. A light in a jewelry store at midnight was suspiciously significant.

His heart leaped when he reached the back and saw the door wide open. He halted again, fearful of entering the black tunnel of darkness opened before him. Danger bristled on every side, and he stepped back as a quick movement came from the doorway.

He had drawn his pocket flashlight and instinctively flung up his arm, but it was a feeble defense against the crushing blow that struck him on the side of the head. As he reeled, a different flashlight shot in his eyes and then swiftly stabbed the night to either side. His assailant was checking to see if Lew had approached alone.

A heavy curtain of black fog swept over his senses, and he fell, but not before he caught one vivid glance of a face in the circle of his own pocket lamp. It was a twisted face with parted lips revealing long, narrow eyeteeth of a dull yellow—fangs that hung bared between parted lips. Even as he fell, Lew vaguely thought of them as a positive clue of identification. They would assist materially in running the robber down, and then his pain-clogged brain knew no more.

*   *   *

Lew shivered, gasped, and sat up shaking. Cold water deluged his face and was running down his shirt. He wiped the drops from his eyes and looked up to find a crowd of men standing over him. One held a bucket, which he had emptied over Lew's head.

He glanced about the faces, and his gaze stopped as he recognized Baker, the village marshal. "The robber?" he questioned breathlessly. "Did you get him? The man with the long, yellow teeth?"

Baker shook his head sternly and glanced at the other men standing in the circle. Lew roused himself to action. "Quick!" he cried. "We must start after him before he gets away. He must have a big start now!"

He struggled to his feet and then stood swaying.

"There wasn't any robber," said Baker in a low voice, and Lew thought he detected a tone of sorrow in that voice.

"Why, what do you mean?" he asked. "I saw him! He struck me on the head as he jumped out the door!" Then he looked around and followed the glance of a man to the ground. Before him lay a small leather wallet whose sides bulged like a clover-bloated cow.

Stooping over, he picked up the bag, thrust his hand past the drawstrings and pulled out a cluster of rings, bracelets and brooch pins. The bag was full of stolen loot from the shop.

Lew flushed, and something cold clutched his heart as he looked around and understood the glances of suspicion he received. They actually believed he had robbed the shop, and that his story of the man with the long, yellow teeth was a ruse to divert suspicion.

* * *

Lew looked pathetically up at his father. He was sitting with bandaged head before the open fireplace, and although his brain still pounded and echoed with strange noises and shooting pains, he had no difficulty understanding the stern admonition he had just received.

"Shand has agreed to not prosecute you, partly because all of the stolen articles were found and partly because of our long friendship. You know I never approved of the company you kept down on the lake, and I always feared those loose companions would get you into trouble. A woods bum who fishes and hunts the year around is no fit company. I can hardly believe that a son of mine would stoop to such an act …"

His voice broke, and Lew shivered involuntarily as he realized it was from anger and stricken pride, not from sorrow or pity for his son.

"But, Father," he cried, "can't you see? There had to be a burglar. Who hit me over the head? Who gathered that jewelry from the shop cases and dropped it in the black bag beside me? It must have spilled from his pocket when he struck me!"

Lew's father shook his head wearily. "I felt the same way until Baker showed me the fallen telephone wire you tripped over as you came from the shop. It lay just before the door, and then you fell forward and struck your head on a pile of bricks. Oh, it is perfectly clear. How many times have I told you the wicked must suffer for their wrongs, that as long as there is a God in Heaven, all evil will be exposed?"

Lew lay in bed that night unable to sleep, reviewing the events of the past twenty-four hours a hundred times. What a change this brief time had made in his hopes and dreams. Sometimes he would sit up suddenly and cry out in exasperation at the stubbornness of those, his own father included, who could believe this mad story of his robbing Shand's shop. And then he would fall back heavily and groan at the dismal future that stretched before him.

A sound caught his ear. Someone was tapping lightly on his window. He arose from bed and walked over to the sash. A screen closed the opening.

"Sssh," came a whisper. "Let me in. It's Charlie."

Lew's heart leaped. Good old Charlie! Here was a faithful friend, a strong heart, staunch and true, who would believe him and help solve the difficulties entangling his way. He removed the screen and Charlie soon stood beside him, gripping his hand in a grasp that numbed his fingers.

"Let's hear all about it, old-timer," whispered Charlie, and Lew repeated the story of everything that had happened since the time he had said "good night" to the bunch at the clubhouse up until the blow on his head had sent him reeling into a world of night.

"Good Lord!" Charlie spat the words out in anger. "What idiots! Didn't they look around for fingerprints or footprints or something to prove another man struck you and escaped?"

"I told them, but the crowd tramped everything up, and Shand had run around his shop a hundred times to check his losses and to figure out how much the insurance would cover, and every possible trace of a clue was rubbed out."

Charlie sighed in exasperation. "Small town hicks, every one of them," he groaned. "Oh, if we could get a real detective down here. But I suppose old Baker won't even send out word to the neighboring towns to watch for suspicious characters."

Then, a new thought struck him. "What do you expect to do, Lew?" he asked anxiously.

Lew hesitated so long Charlie began to think he had not caught the question.

"What can I do?" he finally groaned. "I hate to stay here and face everybody who believes I'm a thief. But if I leave, most of them will be certain I'm guilty."

Charlie straightened up with a trace of excitement in his voice. "It's hard either way, but as you won't improve things by staying, suppose we take that auto-camping trip we have planned for years?

"I was so sure you would see it this way I went ahead and bought that six-cylinder car Newt Harris has been trying to sell me. It's a good old car for a 1923, and I paid just three hundred even. Come, we'll pile the duffle in and light out for new country in the morning."

Charlie's eyes shone with excitement, and Lew's shoulders ceased to sag. His face brightened, too.

"Wouldn't that be great?" he cried. "Just think of us, regular gypsies on the trail, no cares, no worries, headed for new hunting and trapping lands. What a wonderful time we'll have. We'll head south as winter comes on!"

Then he dropped back and the light faded from his eyes. "If this thing only hadn't happened," he muttered quietly, almost to himself.

There was one thing worrying Lew more than the rest, and Charlie thought he could guess what it was.

"I must see Lucille tomorrow," Lew finally said. "Funny she didn't call me today. If she thinks …" he stopped suddenly.

Charlie laid a hand on his shoulder. "Of course she'll think just the same as I do," he assured heartily. "I'll go now. But don't forget we pack the duffle early," and then he swung lightly through the window.

Lew hesitated for hours before he ventured out on the street in the morning. Charlie came over once to urge immediate preparations for the trip, but Lew put him off. He was dreading the ordeal of facing his friends and discovering by their actions who believed in him and who did not.

He felt like a stranger as he emerged from the yard and turned slowly towards the business blocks of town. A slender girl in a fresh morning dress approached, and Lew started forward and then stopped, his heart thumping loudly. Would Lucille believe him guilty of this preposterous charge? Or would she stand by him through a test such as this?

Lucille approached airily, her long stride disclosing a bit of bared knee above rolled stockings. She looked calmly at Lew and then passed as though he were a tree growing beside the curb.

A sharp pain cut through his chest as he realized the truth. For a moment he was weak and dizzy, then his natural sense of fairness took possession of his senses and his anger rose, slowly but steadily gaining momentum.

"The little shrimp!" he thought. "High-hatted me proper, didn't she? And only last Sunday she was asking when I was going to settle down steady so we could be married!"

By the time he reached Charlie's house he was downright mad. Charlie was out in the alley tuning up the car. It was a big, roomy sedan with plenty of speed and power, and Lew thrilled as his mind suddenly pictured them whizzing away through the country, dependent upon nothing but their own abilities and desires. Lew was decidedly temperamental. His mind was capable of lightning shifts, and one was occurring now.

"Let's go!" he cried. "The quicker we get out of this one-horse town the better. I told Dad I might go away for a few months, and for once in his life, he agreed with me."

"That's the stuff!" Charlie declared. "I'll have things fixed up and ready in an hour."

"I met Lucille on the street just now," Lew replied with a chuckle, "and if I didn't know just how strong-minded she is, I'd say she had suffered a lapse of memory. Didn't seem to remember who I was."

Charlie caught eagerly at the note of humor in Lew's voice. He had been fearing that Lew would be badly hurt, for he knew Lucille and had expected this rejection. "In a week," he prophesied, "you'll forget her, too."

They rolled out of town at noon. The car hummed smoothly, and the landscape slipped by with refreshing speed. At five o'clock, Lew, who was driving, looked up from the wheel and remarked, "It's about time to locate a camp; see anything favorable?"

"Right ahead," said Charlie, pointing to an arched gateway that covered a cinder road. It led back into a grove of trees. Across the arch in foot-high letters they read: *Free Camp Ground—Welcome.*

"Attaboy!" said Lew, as he turned in. The day had been hot and the road dusty, and they saw with satisfaction the neat brick building labeled "Showers/Lavatory." Another structure had a wide porch on which sat a row of gas stoves ready for the grub wrangler who would contend with travel-stimulated appetites. A few tents already were scattered through the grove.

They chose a level site, pitched their own tent, made up the beds and then visited the showers. Refreshed and clean, Charlie lugged the cooking kit over to the stoves, fried ham and eggs and then made coffee.

Lew examined their car's tires. "Old bus is holding up fine," he remarked. "Those tires should last us a couple thousand miles more, and by that time, we should have a paying trapline staked out."

As they ate, a small coupe drove in, and two girls tumbled out. They apparently were crossing the continent alone, because a wide banner across the back of their car proclaimed their intention of reaching the Pacific, or, as the banner read in somewhat plain words: "Bust!"

"Sure would be shameful for anything like that to happen to such adventurous girls," Lew remarked. "When I get this sugar roll finished, I'll walk over and see if I can help them make camp."

He didn't stay long. In less than a minute he returned with a rueful grin. "No doubt of those two making it to wherever they've headed," he said. "They told me sweetly but firmly to mind my own business."

"You can't be every flapper's sugar baby," Charlie replied with a grin of his own. Then he cast an appraising glance skyward. "I believe we're going to get a storm tonight. I'll double-stake the tent. It's a small one, but I don't want it tumbling down on us when the ground softens with rain and the wind jerks on the stakes."

Charlie's weather eye proved good. In the night, a sudden gale swept through the little grove, driving a thick sheet of rain before it.

Most car campers are indifferent about the matter of driving tent stakes firmly in the ground and of ditching the edges of a tent. Charlie and Lew were camping in a low shelter model, properly rigged, and the wind did not find enough resistance to cause them any trouble. But several of their fellow campers were not so lucky.

There were a few short cries from the women, exclamations of impatience from the men, and Lew and Charlie poked their heads out in time to see several tents go over. It was a moment of confusion approaching chaos. Those who had searchlights flashed them about. Others pounded at heaving stakes and braved the scudding rain in attempts to hold down the canvas.

"Look at the 'women's rights' tent," shouted Lew. It was swaying and toppling dangerously. A muffled shriek came from inside, the door flap flew hastily open, and out rushed both girls. Then they turned, grabbed the tent, and held on grimly.

"Whoopee!" cried Lew, as a vivid bolt of lightning rent the night. "They're camping in nighties!" Lew was enjoying a little manly revenge for the way he had been rebuffed, first by Lucille back at home and then again earlier that evening by these girls, too. He applauded each time lightning illuminated the camp. Even in these brief flashes, Charlie could see the witheringly angry glances the fair campers shot their way.

The wind ceased almost as quickly as it came, and Charlie dragged the protesting Lew back inside. "Those girls will murder you in the morning," he warned. "And I wouldn't blame them, either."

But they did not wait for such an opportunity. The boys heard a car roll out first thing in the morning, and some time later, when they started out to rustle breakfast, Lew exclaimed, "Why, our fair neighbors are gone! It was their car we heard pull out so early. That's too bad. I was hoping we could trail along with them a while. I wouldn't mind another rainstorm, if they were camping beside us."

"Shut up!" said Charlie good-naturedly. "I'm ashamed of you. Hustle up with that pail of water if you want any breakfast."

They made excellent time that day. Charlie looked down at the odometer. "An even two hundred miles since morning," he said contentedly. "Not bad."

He stretched out an arm and pointed ahead. The car had just climbed to the crest of a steep hill, and before them the road descended and wound through a timbered valley. Off to the right they saw the silver sparkle of water. No houses or fields were visible. "Who would ever suspect there was anything like this just a day and a half from home?"

"It's a paradise for dusty campers," grinned Lew.

Charlie threw the car into second gear and descended easily. At the bottom, he turned off towards the timber, following a dim road between the trees. The timber opened up, and they halted on the riverbank in a small clearing.

"Last one in's a rotten egg!" yelled Charlie. Shoes and clothes poured out on the grass, and both made a flying leap into the water. They splashed about and then crawled up on the grass.

Then they dressed in a leisurely manner, dragged out the tent and built a fire. "Those tourist camps are OK," said Lew, "but give me a camp like this every time."

The sun sank behind the hills, and Charlie, leaning back against a tree with coffee bowl in hand, sighed in sheer contentment. "I'd like to do this the rest of my life," he said.

Lew looked up with a quizzical look. "I believe we have neighbors over there. I thought I heard chopping when we were in the water. Wonder if I should go over and get acquainted?"

"You didn't have very good luck before," said Charlie dryly. "Plenty of time for that. Let's rest in peace for a while."

Charlie did not dream that his simple words had changed the future that lay before them. If Lew had started out to find the neighboring camp, their course on the morrow would have led them back home and not over the hundreds of rough miles that separated them from Big Thunder.

But fickle Fate held the packet of sealed orders in her hand.

"Gosh, Charlie," Lew said. "It's funny. But I never asked you yesterday where we were going. Where are we headed?"

"Who knows?" said Charlie easily. "I'm just enough of a fatalist to believe our future course is already shaped. Our part is merely to follow the trail and let Fate turn us to the right or left as she wills." Then he grinned. "I'm ready and waiting for a sign now!"

And, as if in direct answer to his words, a pistol shot rang out through the timber, followed in quick succession by two more.

Chapter 2 – The Man of Mystery

Lew and Charlie leaped to their feet before the three shots had ceased to echo across the hills that walled in the valley.

"It's too late for anyone to be hunting," said Lew.

A shrill cry broke from the timber ahead. Then a man's voice cursed, and there was a trampling in the brush. Charlie grabbed a gun from the car and cried, "Come on!"

They burst through the brush and ran swiftly towards the voices. A loop of stream lay before them; they cleared it with a single leap. Now a tiny blaze of a campfire guided the way, and they emerged into another clearing in which stood a battered flivver and a ragged tent.

Beside the fire a man lay moaning. Charlie stooped over him and saw he was quite old, his hair and beard white, his face wrinkled and cut into lines by years of wind and weather.

Lew pointed to a bloodstain that spread slowly on his shirt. "Just missed the heart," he said.

The man opened his eyes and stared around wildly. "Stop them!" he cried feebly. "Bring them back!" And then he spoke wearily. "All my years of work gone in a minute. My samples, all the notes …" his voice trailed off to unintelligible sounds.

Leaning close, Charlie caught the final muttered words "millions," "buried," and then "clay."

Then the old man struggled and sat up to cry, "Kill Clinch! Knock his long, yellow teeth down his throat!" and fell over unconscious.

Lew started at the last words. "Did you hear?" he asked tensely. "Long, yellow teeth? I believe he's talking about the man who robbed Shand's jewelry store and knocked me out!"

Charlie nodded. "We must get this man to a doctor as fast as we can. I don't know whether we can do anything for such a wound. If he dies, we never will know who this Clinch is. Help me!"

As they picked up the old man and started back to their camp, they heard a motor bark out in the timber and then a rapid clash of gears. The attacker was escaping, but they could not abandon the old man to try to stop him.

They bundled their tent in the rear of the car, laid the wounded man on it, and then started driving carefully back to the road. Their map located a town a few miles ahead. Lew sat in the rear to watch and ease their patient over the rough patches.

The man was so quiet the first few miles he began to fear he had passed

The Adventures of Lew and Charlie

away. "Step on it!" said Lew. "We must get there quickly!"

Charlie stepped on the gas pedal, and soon village lights came into sight. They hailed a solitary policeman on the street, told briefly what had happened, and asked for the nearest physician. The officer climbed in to point the way.

The boys paced anxiously in the waiting room while the doctor was examining the wounded man. Finally, after what seemed to be hours, he emerged with good news.

"Just a nasty flesh wound," he assured them. "He is a pretty hardy man for his age, and unless something unexpected sets in, he should come around in less than a week."

They explained briefly the circumstances. The doctor nodded. "He seems well supplied with money for a hobo camper. Officer Kennedy has taken charge of his personal effects. We'll send him over to the hospital at once. I believe if you come around at noon you will find him able to talk. He seems to be suffering from some sort of shock or disappointment as much as from the bullet. It drilled a clean hole through his shoulder. I saw men in the war get up and fight the next day after such a wound."

The boys drove back to their camp. They moved the old man's car and meager outfit by their own. Sleep was impossible. They sat gazing into the fire, speaking briefly between deep spells of thought.

"What does it all mean?" Lew finally asked.

Charlie shook his head. Then he grinned. "It appears Fate has tied up the threads of our lives with this old man's. All we can do is play the game until the knots are untied in the future. But I believe we are on the track of the man who committed the robbery for which you stand accused. I hope you get your hands on his windpipe. Too bad he got away tonight, but we'll learn something tomorrow that will help us run him down."

"Remember," Lew mused, "the old man said 'them.' There must have been at least two of them, and they stole something from the old man after they shot him. I wonder if any of the shots we heard came from the old man's gun? I hope he winged one of the brutes."

Then Charlie replied thoughtfully, "What did he mumble when he lay there? Something about 'millions' and 'buried,' wasn't it?"

"Yes," Lew replied. "Unless he was batty from the shot, he must have something of great value stowed away. Sounds baffling, doesn't it? I suppose, though, it will turn out to be nothing. The only place such mysteries happen is in stories."

"Anyway, we'll know more about everything tomorrow," decided Charlie. "I believe I'll turn in and rest, even if I don't sleep."

In the morning, the boys packed their outfit, stowed the belongings of the wounded man in his ancient flivver, and Lew drove it behind Charlie back to town. Here they stored it in a garage, and then they waited until word was brought down of the patient's condition.

"Everything's coming along fine," Doc Martin told them. "He is sitting up and asking for you. He doesn't remember very clearly about last night, only that a couple of good Samaritans brought him in, and he is very grateful for it."

The man made a contrasting picture from the last time they saw him. He sat propped up on pillows, an old man but still a hardy one, with clear skin and kindly eyes. He stretched out both hands as Lew and Charlie entered the room somewhat diffidently and approached the cot.

"It was fine of you to take care of me last night," he said. "I am Dale Harmon, from Skelton County in the Cold Water Mountains."

"We only did what we'd expect from anyone else," explained Charlie. Then he introduced Lew and himself and added a few words, explaining how they came to be camping in the woods last night.

Lew was burning with impatience and finally burst out, "You spoke of a man with long, yellow teeth. What about him? Who is he? I've a strong reason for getting my hands on him, too!"

Dale Harmon's eyes clouded. "Yes," he said, "I must tell you about last night. But first, tell me what you know of Clinch Deering."

"I don't know him by any name," said Lew, and then he told the story of how he had caught a man with long, yellow teeth robbing Shand's jewelry store, how he had been struck over the head and awoke to find himself somehow implicated. His voice grew bitter as he repeated the tale of the turning point in his young life.

"That was Clinch, without a doubt," Harmon said. "He has been following me for a week, waiting for a chance to rob me. I suppose his money ran short in your town and he tried robbery to get back on his feet."

After a long pause, Harmon declared, "Good! Then we've both got a score to settle with him! And with that scoundrel Spad who obeys his beck and call like a pup. It's a long story, too long to tell now when time presses as it does. I should be on my way home this minute!"

He covered his face with his hands for a moment. "You must know that those wretches want something of mine very badly—several things, in fact—for I suppose I must include Anne among them."

Then he looked up with fire in his eyes. "But with two strong, young men behind me, I can beat them!" he cried. "Join me, and you may not only clear your name and put Clinch behind bars where he belongs, but win a reward that will make you rich for life! Go on ahead of me to the mountains and help Anne guard the valley gap. I swear I will share equally with you when I return."

Charlie looked at Lew in doubt. Dale caught this glance and spoke again. "And if you like to hunt and trap, there is the whole length of Big Thunder Valley that I've guarded for twenty years. Not a trap has been set between its cliffs in that time."

Then he pulled a photo from under his pillow. "That is Anne, and those scoundrels are speeding back to mistreat her. There is no law in Big Thunder. She will be helpless. Oh, you can't refuse me!"

"We'll go," said Charlie simply.

Dale drew a pocket map out on the bed and rapidly traced off a route for their guidance. "You are woodsmen; you can follow the old Hog Back Trail over the mountain. It's forty miles shorter than the auto trail Clinch will use. Here," he sketched swiftly, "is the cabin. Anne is waiting for me there. Oh, why did I leave her alone? If I could start at once … but they say it'll be three days before I can leave this hospital bed."

He resumed his instructions. "Leave your car here," he made a mark on the map. "That's Hawley's ranch; they are friends of mine."

"Don't worry," soothed Charlie. "We will beat those devils. When they come ambling up to the gap we'll be waiting for them. Leave it to us, Mr. Harmon. Stay here, and get back your strength."

"Don't forget the …" he broke off quickly. "Don't forget … you will be well repaid."

"We'll settle that part later," said Lew. "All I want is the chance to give this Clinch guy a sock over the head like I got, only about three times harder."

They turned to go, but Harmon called them back. "The password," he whispered quickly, "to show Anne you have really come from me and that she can trust you." Then he whispered in Charlie's ear a single word.

"God grant you speed" were his parting words.

The boys walked silently down to the street and halted before their car.

"Now what are we getting into?" asked Charlie thoughtfully.

"I don't care, just so I get my hands on Clinch!" shot back his partner. "And," he continued, grinning, "that Fate you're so fond of telling me about is leading us straight to the Cold Water Mountains. Who are we to question Fate? There's no stopping now!"

"Jump in," commanded Charlie. "If Fate leads to the mountains, let's make it snappy!" He shot the car into motion with three sharp bursts of speed as he passed from one gear to the next.

"A pretty girl, wasn't she?" enthused Lew as they sped along. "Sounds like some sort of a fur pocket, too, he's got locked up down there. Wonder if he was loony from last night, or was he talking straight? Wouldn't I like to squat down in such a valley as that!"

"You're forgetting the reward he will share with us," reminded Charlie.

"Oh," Lew dismissed with a wave of one hand, "he just has some sort of a mine staked out. I've heard of those mountains. I guess there is nothing richer than a little lead and zinc."

"You forget there's a diamond mine in these parts," again prompted Charlie. "The only one in the world still operating outside of South Africa."

Lew also waved this bit of information away airily. "We won't stumble on any diamond mine, no matter what Fate is holding for us. She saves such things as that for better-looking birds than we. Oh, I almost forgot. What was the password he whispered in your ear? You know—to show Anne we really came from her father."

"Ferruginous," said Charlie quietly.

"Ferrug ... what's that?"

Charlie turned and looked at him queerly. "Ferruginous refers to a certain clay in which diamonds are found," he said.

Lew's jaw dropped at that. Then he whooped aloud. "Ride 'em, cowboy!" Step on her, old-timer! Knock that flivver off the road! Fate has given us the right of way!"

The mud-spattered car ahead ground along noisily. Two men were seated in front, and about the sides hung the usual equipment of camping tourists. Charlie pulled around beside them with a spurt of speed. The driver turned to look at them and curved his lips in a half snarl, half grimace. As Lew met his gaze, the man's upper lip curled back in a snarl that exposed two long, snagly, yellow eyeteeth.

"That's him!" yelled Lew. "Clinch! The man with the teeth."

Completely losing his head, Lew bounced up and down in the seat like a child. Apparently, Clinch heard him, for he suddenly crowded over, forcing Charlie into the ditch. Then the other car shot ahead with renewed speed.

Charlie twisted the steering wheel as their car's rear wheels slid onto slippery grass. He braked hard to prevent a turnover as Lew shouted threats at the other departing car.

"Jump out and push," ordered Charlie. "We can't do anything until we get out of this ditch."

He snapped the car back into first gear and turned the wheel slowly. Lew grunted and strained with all of his strength. It was just enough to turn the balance and start some tire traction. The car rolled back onto the road, Lew jumped in, and Charlie opened the throttle wide.

The men ahead had a quarter-mile start and were driving like race veterans. Charlie hung grimly to the wheel, nursing the speedometer to sixty, past sixty, and there it hung. Fortunately, the road was wide and straight. They passed several oncoming cars whose occupants stared at them in surprise. One motorist leaned out and shouted what Lew took to be a warning, but of what he couldn't understand.

They gained steadily on the car ahead. Gradually, its outline became clear, and they could see both men leaning forward, "pushing on the wheel" as Charlie termed it, in an attempt to crowd more speed from the motor.

Closer and closer they drew, a hundred yards, fifty; now they could hear the man beside Clinch threaten. Suddenly, he turned back to face them and Lew yelled a warning, "He's going to shoot!"

He had thrust a high-power rifle over the back of the seat and now laid his fury-inflamed face alongside the stock. Charlie gripped the wheel, and in doing so saved them from a disastrous spill.

The rifle cracked, and a second report followed as a front tire, pierced by the bullet, blew and nearly threw them sideways off the road. Only Charlie's iron grasp on the wheel saved them from turning over.

"Good shot," was his only comment.

The car slowed, and he applied the brakes. It was no use trying to pursue with a flapping tire, and the car ahead disappeared in a cloud of dust.

"We have to hurry," Lew said, jumping out and grabbing tire wrench, jack and spare. It is doubtful if any mechanic in the auto pits at the big races ever made a quicker wheel change. Lew gave the lugs a final twist as Charlie kicked down the jack. "Let's go!" both exclaimed in unison.

A rumble from behind brought them both around. A motorcycle cop was bearing down at top speed. His brakes screeched as he stopped alongside.

"Here's the man to help us," cried Lew joyfully.

But when the officer dismounted, he thrust a belligerent jaw at them. "What do you think this is, anyway? A speedway? You birds know you were hittin' sixty-five back there?"

"If we weren't, it's only because this old bus can't go any faster," said Charlie. "We're chasing two thieves, but they shot out our front tire and now they're getting away."

"You can catch them!" burst in Lew. "Two men in a flivver! Your cycle will catch them in five minutes."

"Think I'm nutty?" the cop said in disdain. "Be a fine thing to send me chasing over the country while you guys beat it off the other way. Back to the office, for youse!" And he motioned grimly for them to precede him back down the road the other way.

They pleaded in vain for him to instead overtake the car speeding the other way. He cut them short and finally ordered complete silence. Charlie looked ruefully at Lew as he backed around and started back.

The officer halted them at a tiny house beside the roadway. Inside sat a whiskered individual of decidedly rural aspect. "Here they be, Justice!" said their captor. "Speeding," he added briefly and sufficiently.

The justice regarded them for a second and then spoke. His words were equally brief and to the point. "Ten dollars!"

Charlie stepped forward and laid a bill upon the pine table.

He jerked the protesting Lew outside.

"Shut up!" he whispered in a low voice. "Can't you see the more you say, the worse off we'll be? When something like this happens pay your money like a good sport and get out as fast as you can. We were speeding all right," he grinned in remembrance. "No use arguing with a justice about that. I know — my father used to be one."

"But now Clinch is miles ahead. We'll never catch him," moaned Lew.

"We'll still beat him to the cabin," Charlie promised. "When we strike that rough trail over the mountain, we'll show them some speed."

They climbed in the car. "I've got a hunch Fate is leading us right after all," resumed Charlie.

"How do you figure?" Lew said impatiently. "It isn't Fate, it's just us. We're what we make of ourselves and our opportunities, and we just missed a swell opportunity to truss up Clinch."

"First thing, you've got to learn to control your wavelength," said Charlie good-naturedly. "You broadcast entirely too much negativity, not to mention tipping off Clinch back there." And this was as near as he ever came to rebuking his companion Lew.

"No use in hurrying now," he continued. "I haven't another ten to spare. Just steady, safe driving from now on."

But a new note had been injected into their mission. They had changed from carefree travelers, indifferent to time or place, into serious adventurers with a destination and time to keep.

Much country was traversed that day. Once, when in a state park, Lew called a sudden halt. "I saw a beaver cutting back there," he said. They stopped and ran back to a small grove of cottonwood that grew beside the steep road bank. Several of the trees were neatly severed and lay upon the ground.

"Look!" cried Charlie. "They are dragging them down to water. The dam can't be far off." In the soft earth they saw a plain trail made by the energetic animals as they dragged in sections of tree.

"There it is!" exclaimed Lew, pointing where a mere trickle of water had been backed up by a series of three dams. A beaver lodge had been started in the first pool, its round, bowl-like top just clearing the water.

"A pair of youngsters must have left the parent colony and are setting up housekeeping," said Charlie. "The busy bee has nothing on these natural engineers who can fell trees just the way they want, build dams and canals to bring in distant timber when the nearby supply is exhausted.

"We owe a lot of the early history of our country to the beaver," he continued. "Their fur drew the Western trappers to explore and open thousands of miles of territory along the Missouri, Colorado and Columbia rivers."

"I'd like to cave in part of that dam and set some No. 4 longsprings in the breaks," said Lew. "But, of course, they are protected. If they weren't, beavers soon would be extinct around here."

They turned back to the road. "I wonder," Lew said, "if there is anywhere left where a fellow can find a strip of virgin trapping, with fur and game as it was in those days?"

Charlie grinned at that. "I have a hunch, old-timer, we are headed for something just like that. I'm banking pretty strong on that man Harmon."

The country got a whole lot rougher after that, with hills increasingly steep and long. They came to realize they were approaching the foothills of the Cold Water Range. The roads were poor and showing little travel. By the end of the fourth day, houses and farms were infrequent, and half a day might pass without their meeting another car.

Finally, they pulled up beside a group of low rambling buildings with the name "Hawley's Ranch" scrawled in brown paint across the gables of the largest.

"The end of the first lap," said Charlie as he stepped out and straightened the kinks from his legs.

Lew knocked at the door. A woman opened it, and he asked if they could leave the car with her, mentioning Harmon's name.

"I have a message for you," she surprised him by saying. It was a telegram, and Lew tore it open hurriedly. It was addressed: "For the two young men who will ask to store their car at Hawley's Ranch."

They read the single sentence: "Harmon delayed account of complications."

"That's tough," commented Charlie. "Guess it's up to us, now."

Chapter 3 – Over Hog Back Trail

Within half an hour, Lew and Charlie had completed arrangements to store their car at the ranch. They also purchased three days' supply of food and packed up two tote bags with the necessary articles for their tramp. They left the ranch, headed for the rough Hog Back Trail indicated on the pocket map on which Dale Harmon had sketched their route.

It was a struggle over rocks and through thickets of brush with green briars that ripped their flesh and clothes. The trail had once been a logging road, but it had grown up during years of disuse, and constant watch had to be kept to follow the dim ruts made in the past by log skids. In spite of their care, they wandered time and again from the trail and then struggled back upon it.

"What a trail!" grunted Lew as he swung a briar away from his face.

"Remember what Harmon said," Charlie replied. "The last half is the worst. That's when we slide down the mountain and land slap up beside a cabin door. I hope Anne won't mistake us for Clinch and turn loose a load of buckshot before we can offer the password."

"It'll be my luck to wear out the seat of my pants on the slide," Lew grunted in reply. "And I've only the one pair, too. Fine figure I'll cut with the lady. Why, Clinch will look like a gentleman compared to us after the briars get through working us over."

"I can't understand why Harmon left his girl alone," reflected Charlie. "And what was he doing up in our state camping in the woods? Those are only two of the things that are puzzling me."

"I'm sure our old friend Fate will clear that up," Lew replied with just a hint of a smile.

A rabbit jumped from underfoot and scurried off through the leaves. Splashes of vivid color marked the passage of red birds through the foliage. Chipmunks scampered over fallen logs, and they could hear the calls of Bobwhite quail from all points of the compass. Then Lew stopped, one foot poised before him. "Listen!" he cautioned.

A new sound had injected itself into the wilderness setting. The faint, irregular staccato of a motorcar exhaust vibrated up from the valley below. It surged and roared, slackened to a standstill, and then roared anew, as though the car fought a rough, steep trail that could only be made by brief bursts of speed and power.

"Ten to one," said Charlie, setting his foot carefully upon the ground, "it's our friend Clinch taking the other trail into the Big Thunder country. My map shows this trail as a shortcut, miles and miles shorter. If we step on her now, we

The Adventures of Lew and Charlie

can easily beat them. A car isn't much faster than feet in these mountains."

Lew shifted the over-under combination rifle and shotgun he carried to the other arm. "Let's go, then," was his only comment, and they plunged ahead with increased speed.

Their path was a steady climb; the grade, while easy, was perpetual, and when they stopped at noon for a hurried meal their leg muscles ached. They gulped the cold food and started on again, striving with every ounce of strength to cut off as many of the miles separating them from the cabin as they could before nightfall.

At seven o'clock, the mountainside was too dark for travel. After supper, Lew and Charlie spread their blankets over a few hastily chopped pine boughs and slept until cold morning dew drifted over the second-growth timber and drenched their faces with tiny beads of moisture. They shook out their blankets, dressed and huddled about a small fire until the sun burst over the hilltops and rolled the shroud of fog headlong down the mountainside. Charlie consulted the map. He reckoned their position as quite close to the summit from which their course led in a sharp descent to the cabin.

"We should be there in time for a late dinner," he said.

The last miles were most difficult. The logging road had faded out long before, and they were now going by compass. It was all a bit uncertain. The trail changed to ledges of solid rock, and the brush thinned down to scraggly pine and cedars. They puffed and panted as they made a final spurt to the top. It was a sharp, jagged ridge of flinty granite. At intervals, three-foot cedar shrubs sprouted from cracks in the rock, resembling, as Lew remarked, "bristles along the spine of a razorback hog." The trail had been aptly named.

At the ridge line, an involuntary exclamation escaped from both.

Before them lay a panorama of wild beauty. The mountain at their feet fell away in precipitous drops, and at the base a narrow thread of silver blue traced the course of Big Thunder River. The valley was long, and behind it lay a series of mountain ridges that increased in height like the steps of a gigantic staircase, each overtopping the adjoining range until the last and most lofty faded into a misty horizon.

Down in the valley, slender columns of smoke rose lazily up through the air like Indian signal fires. These marked the scattered cabins of the hardy mountain men who comprised the sparse population of Cold Water Range.

"It's wonderful!" breathed Charlie. "I understand now why folks cling to the pioneer life in these places in spite of the hardships. This is a masterpiece by the Greatest Artist of them all."

"Someone's climbing up from the valley!" exclaimed Lew. Charlie listened and also heard the unmistakable click of boots on granite. A loosened pebble rattled down the slope, and the figure of a man emerged from among the piles of rock below.

"I wonder what his business might be," mused Charlie, as they watched the man climb directly towards them. The tall mountaineer carried a rifle over his arm, and he panted lightly from exertion. He looked up, saw the boys, and hailed, "Howdy! Right smart climb up from Big Thunder."

"How far down is that?" Lew asked.

"About a mile, but you can't get to the river from here. I've lived in these parts for thirty years, and every time I hunt, I look for a path down the cliff to the water, but there ain't none."

"You mean we can't get down in the valley from here?" asked Charlie.

"I reckon you can if you've got wings, but not without them. It's a straight drop six or seven hundred feet on all sides. The only way is the narrow gorge at the head, and Old Man Harmon has blocked that with his cabin."

"Who's Old Man Harmon?" asked Charlie, feigning ignorance to fish about for any information he might gather.

"I think he's plumb nutty, same as a lot more about here think," the man replied. "I've heard talk of him having some sort of a mine staked out in the gorge, which is why he don't let no one inside. He homesteaded the valley, so I reckon he's a right to shut us out. And some say he has a secret tunnel or stairway up here from the river, for he's been seen on the ridge right where you're standing, and it's forty miles around by the other trail. I don't pay no 'tention to such, but man, I'd like to set some traps down there. Nary a trap has been set along Big Thunder since the day Harmon squatted in the doorway. I reckon there's fur dying of old age along those banks."

He licked his lips enviously at the thought. "You boys hunting, I reckon?" he asked.

"We're on vacation," said Charlie. "We'll climb down and have a look at the river from the cliff top, anyway."

"If you do, there's one place to step mighty careful," warned the mountaineer. "Right on the edge of the cliff there is a big sinkhole piled nigh full of loose rock. I've peeked down among those stones, and it's all hollow underneath. They're wedged and jammed up in the opening of the sinkhole, and someday there's going to be an all-fired crash when they bust loose and tumble down. Old Man Harmon will sure think all heck's broke loose, then. So keep off of them stones. They're black and sort of scorched, like they'd been burnt a long time ago, so you can't miss them."

He pulled up the straps of his overalls, settled the rifle on his arm, and nodded briefly. Then he started back down the ridge behind with long, loose-jointed strides.

"Say, I'm glad he happened along," said Lew. "Otherwise, we might have stumbled right in that mess of loose stone. Sounds like a man-trap, doesn't it?"

Charlie looked at him and grinned. "That's exactly what we are going to do. Those loose rocks are the door to Harmon's secret trail up from the river. It's marked down on this map. Here, look what he wrote."

Lew examined the drawing. There was a cross labeled "loose stone" and a tiny arrow pointed right to its center. Harmon had written "entrance to cave" in small script.

Lew shivered. "I don't much fancy climbing down there, but suppose we hustle and look it over. Time then to decide what we should do."

After a half hour of rapid descent, Charlie pointed ahead. "There it is!"

Before them sat round, blackened stones covering a rough circle perhaps fifty feet across. Instead of a heaped-up mound as both had expected, the rock had sunken to a saucer depression. It resembled a gigantic whirlpool. Charlie stepped gingerly to the edge.

"There's an opening somewhere, but it looks mighty dangerous to poke around here. If what the man back on the ridge said is true, this is a poised landslide ready to let go anytime."

They slowly circled the rock but could discover no opening.

"It looks as though we must step out on her," said Lew. "What does Fate say about things, now? I'd appreciate knowing whether we're coming back alive or whether we'll be buried under half a mountain of rock if we happen to touch off the trigger that is holding this stuff up."

He picked up a stone and idly threw it off into the brush. A rabbit scurried out and headed straight for the inverted arch of stone. It disappeared down the very center.

"That's the doorway, I'll bet anything," said Charlie. "Old Bunny has shown the way. Now, if we're game enough to follow into a place Dale Harmon has doubtless climbed many a time, we can reach the valley in an hour."

"If we're game!" retorted Lew. "I'll show you!" and he walked steadily for the center. Charlie followed. Both stepped carefully, and both confessed later they expected any second to be buried in a tumbling, crashing avalanche of stone. But the rocks never quivered, and when they reached the sunken center they saw a slanting burrow, much like the mouth of a wolf's den. It was barely large enough for a man to squeeze through.

Charlie tightened his belt. "I'm going first," he said, and before Lew could stop him, swung his feet into the hole and slid down. Lew followed. They slid and wriggled deeper until the burrow widened abruptly and they emerged into a wide cavern or grotto. Charlie looked overhead.

"The mountaineer was right. Look! The rock is jammed into the mouth of this sinkhole or cave, held in place by a single keystone. There must be a thousand tons piled up, and one small stone is holding it all."

They descended twenty feet more and saw before them a wide, high cave that ran obliquely down toward the valley of Big Thunder. The sides glistened with lime stalactites hanging like gleaming icicles, and more water dripped from open rifts in the rock. There was just enough light to see dimly ahead.

"That pile of loose stone has laid there centuries while this cave was hollowed out underneath by seeping water," said Charlie. "It gradually wedged down into a compact mass and supported itself the same as an arch of brick will hold up a building. The cave has slowly enlarged until the rocks have sunk down like a saucer. I imagine they were heaped up by volcanic activity before they settled. That is why they are so dangerous. It wouldn't take much to break up the formation and bring them tumbling down into this cave."

"For Heaven's sake, let's go," said Lew. "I don't enjoy standing here thinking about getting buried alive under half a mountain. I hope that rabbit steps easy when he crawls back out."

They started down. The rock was slippery, and every step had to be made with caution. Down, down the cave led, sometimes dropping straight for a dozen feet, and sometimes running on the level for short lengths of gallery-like form. They dropped over the breaks, hanging by their hands until they were sure they would land safely on a ledge underneath. At one of these drops Lew pointed to a rough series of steps cut into the rock. "Look!" he cried. "It's Harmon's stairway, sure enough. I'll bet we could have found steps at every drop if we had just looked for them."

They reached a place where the cave branched into forks that reached away at right angles. They hesitated, uncertain which to follow. Finally, they selected the right-hand passage and walked carefully, for the light faded and soon they traveled in near-darkness. A sheer wall loomed up before them.

"We picked the wrong way," said Charlie. "This is just a blind alley. No wonder it got dark."

Lew stumbled over an object on the ground. Picking it up, he saw he was holding a shovel. "Somebody has been digging here. Let's look around."

He stepped forward, his foot plunged into space, and he fell straight into the gloom. He cried out sharply and flung an arm back. Charlie caught it, and Lew's full body weight jerked him down on his face.

It all happened in a fraction of a second.

Lew dangled over the edge of a precipice, and Charlie lay stretched full-length on the very brink, clutching him desperately by the wrist. "Dig your heels in someplace," he panted.

Lew kicked frantically, but it was smooth and slick. "No use," he said.

"Better let me drop, old man. I don't want to drag you down with me."

"Be still!" Charlie grunted, and putting forth every ounce of his prodigious strength, he began to drag Lew bodily straight up inch by inch. It was a wonderful feat of muscle. He could only spare one arm, for his other had to brace them both on the edge.

An inch at a time, he pulled up Lew until he got his free hand on top and helped sustain his own weight.

"Hurry!" panted Charlie. "My arm's giving out!" Lew pulled desperately and then, with a final Herculean jerk, Charlie deposited him on the rock. They lay panting for a minute, recovering their breath.

"Thanks!" said Lew simply.

"Shut up!" said Charlie gruffly. "I'm going to drop a match over the edge and see how deep it is."

The tiny blaze flickered down until it rested upon the bottom, flared with a last effort, and died out.

"Forty feet!" said Charlie grimly. "Did you see those half-burned pine knots down there? Somebody has been working that pit, probably digging. I wonder if this is the reward Harmon promised us? A mine, I suppose."

"It came near being a grave for me," said Lew shakily.

They stood up and started back. "Suppose it's lead?" Lew asked. "I know both lead and zinc are in these mountains."

Charlie hesitated a minute and then said, "Diamonds are mined from clay pits, Lew. Harmon is an old man, and he is probably suffering from delusions on this fortune business, but stranger things have happened. But if there is anything down there, it will keep, that's certain. Our job is to beat Clinch and his partner to the cabin and then stand them off. It would be a tough job for a girl alone. Let's go!"

They retraced their steps to the fork and started down the other branch. The grade smoothed out, and the going got easier. "I hear running water," Lew declared, his keen hearing again picking out the slightest sound before Charlie could detect it.

They stopped, and Charlie also heard the faint sound of water tumbling over a rocky bed. "It's Big Thunder! We're nearly out of this cave."

"Can't get out any too quick for me," Lew replied. "I haven't forgotten all those rocks up at the top. The flesh along my backbone has been crawling every step I've taken. When we leave here, I'm going to vote for the long way around as our route home."

The passage narrowed into a mere slit. The rocky roof shot upwards, and they walked through a tall, open vein in the rock with a bright patch of sunlight beckoning them forward. The last few feet of opening shrank to a foot across, and then they squeezed out into the open.

They stood in Big Thunder valley at last, pumping in deep breaths of fresh woods air. Before them ran the river, rushing through foaming rapids. The cave behind was nearly concealed with cedar shrubs, and from a distance resembled merely a curve in the rocky cliff.

Looking up at the overhanging cliffs on both sides, Lew said, "The old man up on the ridge was right. It would be hard to drop in here without wings. It's a natural bottle, and Harmon has built his cabin for the cork. Which way do we go?"

"Upstream," said Charlie. "The map shows the river rising some five miles ahead, and the cabin should be close. Slick up, Lew, if you're going to make a hit with the girl. You look somewhat mussed since I jerked you out of that pit."

They started up the river. "Here's a path," said Charlie. "We might as well follow it."

Lew bent over and examined the trail. He whistled in surprise.

"It's a path, all right, but do you see what made it? It's a regular beaten trail made by fur animals. Look! Here's a coon, and there went a possum. I think this was a fox, and I know those tracks are mink. A regular trail of fur!

"They must be so thick they need a traffic sign at intersections!" He laughed excitedly.

"We've got to get that box of traps over the mountain before cold weather starts. I've read of fur pockets and have heard fellows talk about them, but I never believed we'd fall into anything like this."

"Calm down," said Charlie. "Remember, two or three animals can make a lot of tracks during a summer. Of course there is fur here, for Harmon never allowed trapping. But …" he started involuntarily as a covey of quail whirred up before them.

Lew pointed to a ripple in the water. "Mink, I'll wager. And here on the rocks are leftovers where some old buck coon has fished. See the mussel shells piled up by his tracks?"

It was hard to withstand the temptation to make a closer examination of the valley, but they knew the necessity of haste and hiked forward.

"The other trail was forty miles around," said Charlie. "Clinch is going in his car. Just as a guess, I'd say we still are beating him by half a day."

They turned around a sharp bend in the river and saw a snug cabin stoutly built of logs. "That's it," cried Lew. "It's built like a blockhouse. I guess we can stand a siege, if we have to."

At that moment, a girl's scream pierced the valley. "We're too late!" cried Charlie. "Clinch must have driven though the night and beat us!"

Chapter 4 – The Girl in the Cabin

Another scream—and Lew and Charlie leaped forward at top speed. They dashed around the cabin and then abruptly halted at the scene before them. A slender, fair-haired girl stood with her back against a log wall. Beside her sat a pail of water dipped from the spring that bubbled up among the rocks fifty yards away, and Clinch stood with one hand gripped on her shoulder and the other waving a pistol. His companion, Spad, leaned against the cabin with a smirk of unholy joy on his face.

As they hesitated, the quick ear of Clinch caught a sound and he whirled, dropping his grasp on the girl and covering them with the revolver.

"Stop!" he called. "One step more and I shoot!"

The boys obeyed. He had the upper hand, and Charlie bitterly cursed the sudden excitement that had possessed them and placed them at this disadvantage. They had acted foolishly. The wise course would have been to steal quietly around the cabin and take a quick look before Clinch discovered their presence.

Clinch grinned as he recognized them.

"So?" he questioned tauntingly. "You butting in again?" Then he menaced them with the gun. "Speak up! How did you get here so quick?"

Charlie opened his mouth to reply, although he afterwards confessed he had no idea whatsoever what he might say. That's when the girl looked back of Clinch and cried, "Quick! Shoot him!"

Lew and Charlie gaped until they realized she was attempting an old stunt, but one which has succeeded many times under similar conditions when the odds were overwhelming. It fooled Clinch. He looked swiftly backwards, squaring his shoulders to meet this new attacker. His gun hand dropped level with his hip, and before he could recover, Charlie's hand flashed under his coat with lightning speed and took his own revolver from its shoulder holster. He leveled this gun in Clinch's face.

"Drop that gun." His voice was low, almost a whisper, but his finger curved dangerously against the trigger. Clinch hesitated, his weapon half-raised. In that brief time he stood considering his chances, but the dead calm in Charlie's eyes and the cold menace of the whispered command unnerved him. He knew as surely as though it had been sworn upon the mightiest oath that to disobey meant death. Charlie's finger was tightening up for the final pull that would release the hammer when Clinch swore helplessly and dropped his gun.

His nerve had left him, and he shivered, endeavoring to shake off the feeling that his heart had been squeezed in an icy grip.

Lew watched Charlie's play, so absorbed in the skill of his companion that he forgot to act his part. A cry from the girl brought him to his senses. He sprang forward and leveled his gun, but it was too late.

Spad had drawn his revolver and now pointed it at Charlie. The girl screamed, causing Spad to flinch, and when his gun cracked, the bullet struck a log inches above Charlie's head, throwing a shower of splinters in his face.

At the same instant, Clinch ducked and, followed by Spad, sprang over the low rock wall that fenced the cabin yard. Both scuttled off towards the gateway of the valley.

Lew shot quickly just as Spad vanished over the wall. They heard him yelp, but he continued at top speed. Lew looked down at the over-under in his hands and declared disgustedly, "I meant to give him the rifle barrel, but I hit the wrong trigger, and all I did was pepper him with shot. Darn these double-barrel combinations, I'm always shooting the wrong load."

He ran to the wall for a rifle shot at the fleeing men, but they darted and dodged, much as jack snipe veer and tack before the gunner, and it was useless to attempt a shot as they darted among the rocks. Lew watched until they vanished in the timbered valley and then turned back to the cabin.

Charlie spoke reassuringly to the girl, who stood trembling and breathless. "I suppose you are Anne. Did those devils hurt you?"

"They only threatened me, but ..." she shuddered. "What he said was bad enough. You came just in time. How did you get into the valley? I've watched the gap ever since Dad left."

"Your father sent us on ahead to help you," answered Charlie. "And we climbed down that devil's chimney of a cave. He gave us a sort of password so you would know we really came from him and that you could trust us."

Then he stooped and whispered the word in her ear.

She smiled sadly. "Did Dad tell you of his life's dream? Why we have lived here alone for so many years? Poor Dad! What a disappointment it will be to him if ..." she stopped, a distant look coming into her misty eyes.

Lew broke into the conversation. "He hinted at some big reward that he would share with us, but what I want most is a hundred steel traps and the word to go ahead in this valley. I never saw so much fur sign in all my life."

"Dad might let you trap this winter, but for years he has allowed no one else inside. You know it has only one entrance, and our cabin guards that."

"How about the lower end where the river flows through?" asked Charlie.

"The river leaves in a number of rapids and a waterfall, and the rock cliffs are just as steep as they are here. An old Shawnee Indian showed Dad the valley and how to climb down through the cave. You guessed its name right. They called it The Devil's Chimney years before we came."

"But what is your father promising to share with us—that is, if you have the right to tell?" asked Charlie.

Anne hesitated a minute. "I know he would not be angry at my telling, not after what you have done for me today. But I don't want you to laugh at him. Dad is old, and while he is quick and wise in many things, I have feared for years that he is a little childish in this one regard. He has brooded and worried over this thing for so long it has affected him.

"His dream is to discover a diamond mine or pit like that one in the southern part of the state. He has searched and dug for years, and every time he finds samples of clay that look like they could contain diamonds, he takes them to men he knows up north and tries to interest them in developing the mine.

"He was sure he had the right clay this time. He came in trembling with excitement and told me our fortune was made. Dad isn't strong enough to dig very far, and he counts on getting outside investors to help. Twice before he had gone north and left me to watch the gap. He keeps an old car at Hawley's Ranch over the mountain.

"But why didn't Dad come back with you?" she asked suddenly. "Is he hurt? Quick! Tell me!"

Charlie calmed her fears and then rapidly told the story of the night they saved Dale Harmon and took him into town. When he mentioned Clinch's part, she gripped her small fists tight against her waist and cried, "I knew he followed Dad. For several years he has tried to worm himself in on our secrets. He is the only one who believes Dad may find a valuable claim in the mountain. The rest all laugh at him."

She flushed at that and hesitated.

"He wants me to marry him," she continued with an involuntary shudder, "and that was why Dad finally ran him off. Today, he came and tried to make me believe Dad had sent him for me. When I refused to go, he threatened to take me by force. I hate him!"

She turned in accusation to Lew. "Why didn't you shoot straight today?"

He had been staring at her in open admiration during her story, but now he turned red and stammered. Charlie stepped forward to cover his partner's embarrassment.

"There is nothing to worry about, now," he assured her. "Your father will be here in a few days, and until he comes, we'll see that nobody molests you. If that pair of gallows-cheats comes back, we'll throw them in the river."

Anne glanced at their worn faces and torn clothing, plain evidence of the hard trail they had just completed. "You must be hungry. Come in and sit down while I cook dinner."

Both grinned happily at the prospect of a real meal, cooked and warm.

As she busied herself between the stove and table, they sat and frankly admired. "A regular thoroughbred," whispered Lew. "Some plucky girl to stay here and hold the fort alone."

She was between eighteen and twenty years of age, and while her features could hardly be termed beautiful, her face shone with perfect health and the calm confidence that is bred in mountain lands where nature still holds first place, where civilization and its catalogue of destroying influences has only a feeble foothold. Her dress was of cheap gingham, but well fitted and neatly made. Lew thought of Lucille. What a contrast. Here was a girl who would stick through anything.

They ate heartily. Mountain climbing works wonders for the appetite, and they cleaned up the plate of hot biscuits and then demolished a platter of eggs. Lew leaned back in his chair and sighed in perfect peace.

"Tell me," he said. "What will our friends Clinch and Spad do now?"

"They won't give up," answered Anne. "They know what Dad hopes to find, for when Clinch wanted to marry me, Dad flamed up and said I would soon be loaded with diamonds and much too good for a hillbilly like him. Poor Dad! I know he has been slaving away in that cave just for my sake."

In her voice they could hear the fears and worries that had crowded her life through the many years in Big Thunder Valley.

"Clinch robbed your father of something on the road," Charlie said. "Could it have been his samples, or anything else that would give a clue to the pit he has worked out there?"

"They probably stole the clay samples and also the records he has kept of his work. I think Clinch expected to find the actual diamonds and not just clay. I feel so sure poor Dad is just following a rainbow I would let them dig around all they wanted if I hadn't promised to keep them out. Nobody must pass the cabin. I promised that."

"We'll stop them," said Charlie with confidence. "You hear, Lew? From now on, one of us stands guard at the mouth of the valley. And next time Clinch gets within gunshot range, have your triggers sorted out right. We can't have any more cutting up like today."

Lew merely grinned, but in his heart he resolved that the next encounter would end differently, and he hoped the opportunity to square himself with Clinch would come soon. Then, looking about the cabin, he saw a fishing rod laid along two wooden pegs. He stepped over and took it down.

"If they bite tonight, we might have a mess of fish," he said.

"When we first came here," Anne said, "there were hardly any fish in Big Thunder. I think the falls at the end of the valley kept them from these headwaters. But Dad caught and brought in a lot of small trout and planted them in the upper river. You'll have luck in any of the deep pools. Dad hasn't fished for months."

Lew walked down to the river. The rod was stiff, the reel rusty, and the only bait he could find was a few worms gathered by overturning old logs. He skewered a couple in long loops on the hook and cast it gently in the water.

Something streaked through the pool and hit the bait instantly. "Wow!" breathed Lew. "He struck like a thunderbolt!"

The reel wheezed, and the fish raced downstream with a determination that took Lew scrambling down the bank. He stumbled along, hopping over rocks, maintaining his balance and a taut line with difficulty.

Straight on the fish sped, and ahead lay a rough ledge of rock. Lew saw it too late to check or turn the trout. The long shape darted over the ledge, and then *snap!* The line parted, sawed in two by the sharp limestone.

Lew sat down on the bank mopping his face.

"That fish knew exactly where he was going," he reflected. "Pretty slick, I'll say. I wonder if there's any more like him in the pool?"

He walked back, tied on another hook, and again dropped the bait easily into the water, this time dangling it enticingly before a large, dark hollow that ran back into the riverbank. Whang! Another bolt of slippery chained lightning struck and then darted downstream. "Aha!" cried Lew. "I'm onto that trick. You'll have to try something new."

He skillfully braked the reel, checking the fish without following it down the bank. Several times he flinched as the line sawed across rock, but the linen strands held, and the fish turned and started back upstream. Lew now had the advantage, and when he coaxed the trout back into the pool he reeled in easily, giving slack only on the most vicious side twists. When he had the line in, he stooped and lifted out a two-pound trout. It was a beauty.

"That first fish must have gone him at least a pound better," thought Lew. "Trout," he said out loud, "I'm afraid you've grown lazy from want of exercise. I'll see that the rest of your family gets some exercise while I'm here."

He cast again, and the fish bit steadily. They were smaller, mostly under a pound, but it took only a few minutes to get a string that would easily satisfy three mountain-air appetites. Lew carried them proudly back up to the cabin.

Charlie was busy making camp. He selected a small, split-log shed that stood forty yards from the cabin right in the very neck of the valley. He regarded it as a post of strategic value.

Anne was watching him with troubled eyes.

"I'm afraid you won't be very comfortable there. I'd like to offer you the cabin, but I'm alone ..." she broke off in confusion.

"My dear girl," assured Charlie, "Lew and I would suffocate in a cabin.

We sleep best when the sky is over us. If you just call us at meal times," he added with twinkling eyes, "that's when the inside of a cabin looks best."

She smiled gratefully at that.

They retired to the shed after supper, and Charlie rolled up a low wall of loose stone against the side that faced the open hills beyond the valley.

"Some bird might try a shot for luck through these walls," he explained. "Sure has been a busy day, old-timer. What do you think of the layout as she stands now?"

"I'm highly in favor of the 'she' part," said Lew emphatically. "Ain't she a peach? Can you imagine any of those paint-smeared dolls back home sticking through everything like she has? Yep," he concluded, "on the whole, I'm pretty well pleased with the deal.

"But what worries me is just waiting for Clinch to strike. We can't set up nights indefinitely. That's where he has the advantage of us. If we could only hunt him down and run him off so far he'd never come back! I would really like to settle down in peace and study out the trapping prospects."

"That's something you can't expect, Lew. Anytime you find a fur pocket as rich as this one seems to be, you'll find competition and trouble. Remember our time up North? Maybe this Clinch wants the fur as badly as the supposed diamonds? Clinch seems far too cunning to be led on a wild goose chase. But I reckon the only thing is to guard the place until Anne's father comes back. It's his valley, and whatever he says goes."

The night passed quietly. Lew and Charlie took turns before the fire, guarding the narrow cleft in the cliffs that offered the only gateway into Big Thunder Valley.

Early the next morning, Lew caught another string of trout. "It's getting too easy," he confessed. "I just flip in the bait and a trout nails it. It makes me laugh when I think how we would sit for hours back home to pull out a single sucker. This valley is sure enough a paradise."

"It's no place for a girl like Anne to be alone, though," returned Charlie. "I want to explore the valley some today. One of us should stay at the cabin, and I don't think you'll kick at the job."

"I'll say I won't," grinned Lew.

Dale Harmon's homestead lay partly outside the valley, but enough of the land was enclosed inside the cliffs of Big Thunder to give him effective control of the entire valley. In past years, he had farmed a few acres behind the cabin, but these had since grown up in hickory and sassafras brush. Both banks of the river were fringed with slender cane.

Charlie walked slowly down into the valley, watching carefully for signs of fur and game. He found plenty. The cliffs were honeycombed with dens, and at the entrances he found unmistakable sign of skunk, fox and possum. Along the edge of the water were coon, mink, muskrat and weasel tracks.

One thing he wanted to settle was if any wolves had denned in the valley. Even one den could make a big difference in the fur supply. There was no stock in the valley except Harmon's cow and chickens, and any wolves would, of course, prey upon the wild furbearers.

He was relieved to find no trace of wolves, but he did make some interesting discoveries. The valley he judged to be five or six miles long and not over five hundred yards at the widest point. In the lower end, the river cut through a steep clay bank, and here Charlie saw a smooth path worn down the slope. It was too steep for a path, really, and when he noticed parts of the earth were still wet, as though something had splashed water up from the river, he knew he had come upon an otter slide.

Otter were scarce this far up from the gulf, but Charlie knew that, occasionally, a pair would follow the Mississippi north and turn up a tributary, eventually settling in wild places like Big Thunder.

The whole valley was an immense, natural fur farm, more than a mere pocket where a trapper might make good catches for a few weeks. Properly handled, it would furnish a lifetime of trapping. As Lew had discovered, the river was full of trout, and Charlie had seen turkey sign near the cliffs. If one could drive in a few deer and let them multiply, an outdoorsman would have everything he might desire.

He retraced his steps back to the cabin.

Nothing had happened during his absence, and two more uneventful days passed. It was nearly time for Anne's father to arrive, and they expected to see him come down over Hog Back Trail any day. No sign of Clinch and Spad was seen. Charlie made a short trip over in the hills near where Anne indicated Clinch had a cabin, but saw no sign of either of their adversaries.

Lew went on sentry duty that night. He strolled back and forth in the narrow gap, wishing the night vigils could stop. It was a lonely, boring job. Charlie lay asleep in the little shed camp. Lew grew more restless, and finally, he walked out of the valley and into the hills beyond. He thought a short walk would help him sleep when his shift was done.

Lew walked on and on until he suddenly realized he had gone too far and should not have left his post unguarded. He turned back when he realized his mistake, but he had taken only a step when a small light twinkled out in the hills. It flashed and disappeared regularly, as though someone was carrying a lantern between brush and timber.

Lew's curiosity overcame his natural caution, which was small enough, anyway, and he started forward to investigate.

The light approached steadily. Lew stopped to listen and fancied he heard voices. He waited and then was sure he heard both voices and footsteps from a number of men. Lew turned to one side and hid behind a boulder. The party advanced and stopped nearly abreast of where he crouched.

The man carrying the lantern held it up to his face, raised the glass and extinguished the light. It was quickly done, but Lew caught a clear view of the face in the small circle of light.

It was Clinch, alright, and behind him were five men.

"Can't use this light any further," he spoke. "Quiet now. Heaven help the one of you who makes a sound. We'll rush those two young fools up there before they know what's happening. Remember, the old man has quarts of diamonds up in the cave. It's share and share alike, men. Only the girl—she's mine. I'll kill the first one who lays a hand on her!"

Lew's heart sank down to his shoes. They were going to rush the gap, and he had left Charlie asleep and helpless. He had deserted his post.

Chapter 5 – The Fight at the Gap

Lew crouched behind the rock, thinking swiftly. He knew he must beat Clinch and his gang to the valley gap or they would catch Charlie asleep and shoot him before he had any chance to defend himself.

He started to creep away, keeping the boulder between himself and the men who stood about while Clinch gave them instructions for the final attack. His only hope lay in absolute silence until he was far enough away to make a dash to the little shed where Charlie slept.

Step by step he eased over the rough hillside, and he was beginning to breathe again when his shoe kicked a loose stone and sent it rattling down the slope. There was nothing to conceal him, and he froze in his tracks.

"What's that?" Clinch asked sharply. "Throw your light over there, Spad!" A thin beam of light cut the darkness and revealed Lew crouching on the open ground.

"Get him!" roared Clinch, and the gang went after Lew, who ran like a rabbit, hugging the ground as close as he could. He had little fear of their shooting him in the dark. In fact, he hoped they would shoot, as it would alarm and awaken Charlie. Fear added to his speed, and he drew away from the older men who pursued. And then, just as he anticipated certain escape, his foot caught on a root and he fell headlong on his face.

For a moment he lay half-stunned, then, as he struggled to arise, Clinch fell heavily upon his back and twisted his arms behind him. He flashed the light in Lew's face and exclaimed, "Why, here's one of 'em now. Ain't we lucky! Our job'll be easy now."

He peered into Lew's face. "I've seen this bird somewhere before. Let me think." Sitting astride Lew's back, he twisted a rope about the boy's wrists.

"I have it!" he cried suddenly. "He's the guy I blackjacked over the head behind the jewelry store!"

The rest of the men laughed at that, and Lew's temper simmered. Clinch jerked Lew to his feet and grinned at him in the light of the electric torch.

"We'll have to leave you here until we settle with the other one up there. Maybe you boys will wish you had minded your own business and stayed clear of Big Thunder."

He turned to one of his companions. "You stay here and watch him, Lem! Set him over behind those rocks, and if he yells or kicks, stick your knife in him. It'll save me the trouble!"

Lem appeared to regard this task with disfavor, but it wasn't the knifing he objected to. "I want to be thar when you get the shiners, Clinch!" he protested.

Clinch snarled at him in savage tones. "I'm boss around here, and if you don't know it now I'll larn you good!" He drew back his arm to strike a backhand blow, and Lem silently turned Lew about and marched him behind the rocks. The rest moved away in silence.

Lew's heart felt like a lump of lead as he stumbled before Lem. He knew it was all up for Charlie. Clinch and his gang were advancing with murder in their hearts, and they were inflamed with liquor. He caught the unmistakable stink of corn whiskey on the man Lem, who silently prodded him from behind.

They sat down on stones. Lem kept a firm grasp on the rope that bound Lew's wrists while a six-shooter dangled comfortably from his other hand.

"Just my luck!" he grunted. "Durn ye! I've got to stay here and watch while Clinch and the rest get all of the diamonds. I've a mind to knock you on the head!"

"If you're worrying about those diamonds," said Lew, "you can calm down. Clinch is going to be badly disappointed when he searches that cave."

Lem regarded him with surprise. "Clinch swore there were bags of stones up thar. I guess Clinch ought to know. He's been hanging around the mouth of the valley long enough to get next to what old man Harmon's doing."

"Harmon has not found a single diamond." asserted Lew convincingly. "All he has ever found is a sort of clay like the stuff diamonds are mined in. Even his daughter says he's grown childish over it. I know, too, for we were both up in the cave and down in that pit."

Lem regarded him doubtfully. Lew sensed the hesitation and struck further. "It's serious business to commit murder—especially for nothing. Clinch will find himself in bad before he sees the last of this. Harmon knows we are down here, knows what Clinch is up to, and he'll have the law running all of you down like hounds after rabbits. You're in dangerous company, man."

Then, playing a hunch, he added, "Do you really want to see that skunk misuse Anne?"

"No-o," hesitated Lem. "Miss Anne was always kind to me. She nursed my wife through a bad chill two summers past. But a man who has starved in these hills all his life will do a lot for the money Clinch has promised. Why, we could move back to Oklahoma and be content the rest of our days."

"But Clinch is only fooling himself, and you, too!" cried Lew. "There are no diamonds in that cave. The only valuable thing Harmon has is a valley full of fur, and a man would have to be pretty bad off to shoot another for the chance to trap!"

"Everyone has always said Harmon was half-crazy," mused Lem.

Hope flooded back into Lew's heart. He was sure the man was won over.

"If what you say is right," Lem continued, "the best thing for me is to get out of here." He stood up to leave, and Lew pleaded, "Cut me loose, first! Then no matter what happens in the gap, I'll swear you were not in on it."

"That's a bargain," said Lem. "If I thought them diamonds was real, I'd stick. That valley was always ourn, and we had the run of it until Harmon came along and blocked the gap. But you've got me convinced, young fellow, and I'm going to get out of here."

He reached over and slashed the rope with his knife. "I never did take much stock in misusing the girl. What are you …" He stopped, his question unfinished, for Lew already had darted off towards the gap.

As he ran, leaping boulders in the darkness, which was now tinged with the gray of early sunrise, Lew prayed that he would not be too late. He ran as he had never run before, and down in his heart was a faint hope that he might, after all, arrive in time. It was a good half-mile to the gap where Charlie slept unsuspecting in the shed.

All was silent about him, and as he ran, the faint hope in Lew's heart grew larger. He dashed ahead with increased speed. And then a volley of rifle shots burst out. He never slackened his stride, but he groaned aloud, "Too late!"

*　　*　　*

Up in the shed, Charlie slept like a log. The fire outside had burned low, casting flickering shadows upon the log wall behind. Charlie shivered in his sleep, stirred, then turned over and opened his eyes. He was cold, and he reached down for an extra blanket. Then a feeling of uneasiness gripped him, and he stood up looking for Lew.

He walked to the door and called sharply, "Lew!" There was no answer, and now Charlie became thoroughly alarmed. He looked up towards the gap and saw something moving among the rocks. It was indistinct, but his sharp eye caught the motion.

Charlie stepped back and seized his rifle. Again he caught a glimpse of something moving through the gap. He crouched in the doorway waiting. Where the deuce was Lew? Had something happened to him?

A faint click of steel warned Charlie of imminent danger. He threw up his gun and fired. A rattle of shots answered, and bullets thudded into the logs about his head. He dropped flat on the ground, straining his eyes to see out in the gray shadows.

Now he knew Clinch was attacking. Out there among the rocks, desperate men were worming their way through like Apaches. Taking advantage of every rock and shadow, they crept forward like snakes, as deadly as mountain rattlers.

Charlie reloaded the rifle, and drawing his revolver, laid it beside him on the ground. It was still too dark to see the advancing men, but he gauged their approach by the slight sounds that reached his ears. He wished for the keen hearing of his partner, but relied instead on his own sharp eye.

Closer and closer came the line of crawling men, and Charlie began to shoot, quick snap shots at every motion and sound. He had little hope of hitting, but if he could hold them back and discourage their approach until day broke, more light would make the shooting easier. He had picked the shed with care and knew it was defensible—as long as the attackers didn't get too close under the waning cover of night.

In spite of his efforts, the approach was steady, relentless. When they were within fifty yards, Charlie grew truly alarmed. They advanced through his fire with a deadly determination that conveyed intent. When close enough, they would rush, and while he might get one or two, it would soon be over. He would have absolutely no chance in a hand-to-hand fight with so many.

Charlie cast a quick glance towards the cabin. What had Anne been doing? She had to hear the rifle fire in the still valley. He saw a light through a narrow window and could picture her watching and listening. The cabin was stout. He must make a dash for it, and once sheltered by the thick log walls, he would have an even shot at holding off Clinch and his gang. To stay here was plain suicide.

He jumped back in the shed, stuffed his pockets with shells, and returning to the door, emptied his revolver rapidly. Then, crouching low, he ran with all his speed towards the cabin.

The attacking party stood and fired when they saw him run. The bullets rattled about, but he kept on, unscathed. Charlie covered those forty yards in seconds, although to him it seemed an age. As he ran he recalled the stories of fire fights he had read, and it seemed as though he lived through all of them as the bullets droned like angry bees all around him.

He breathlessly shouted as he reached the door. It swung open, and he dove inside. It closed quickly behind him, and Anne stood with her back against it, regarding him with wide, frightened eyes. Charlie turned and peered out the window that faced the gap. Five men were running in a wide skirmish line towards them.

"Have you seen Lew?" he asked as he thrust his gun forward. He fired twice without waiting for an answer. "Ha!" he exclaimed with satisfaction. "I winged him!"

One of the attackers stumbled and fell. The rest, noting the accuracy of the shot, stopped and dropped, concealing themselves among the rocks.

Anne answered with another question, "Don't you know where he is?"

Charlie shook his head. "Something must have happened. I woke up, and he was gone. It's lucky the fire burned low, because the cold is the only thing that woke me. They'd have got me sure if it hadn't."

He stepped back from the window as a volley struck the logs. "Back up!" he commanded. "Some of those bullets may be high-power enough to come clear through the logs. Go to the other room, and lie flat on the floor."

But Anne shook her head. "You may need me to load the guns," she said simply and then sat on the floor beside him. He turned the shells out of his pockets and quickly showed her how to put them in both rifle and revolver.

The men out in the rocks were planning another move. He could hear brief calls and low commands, and Clinch seemed to be exhorting them for a fresh attack.

"They're going to rush us," said Charlie. "But this cabin will be a harder nut to crack than an open shed." He leveled the gun and waited in grim silence.

A shrill whistle sounded, and four men leaped to their feet and dashed towards the cabin. Charlie fired twice without effect. The light was still bad, and they ran in a swift zigzag that defied accurate sighting. He reloaded and stood waiting before the door.

The blows of an ax shook the heavy slabs. He tried to fire through it, but Clinch, wielding the ax, stood back behind the thicker cabin wall slashing at the crude wooden hinges that pinned the door in its frame.

Charlie laid down his rifle, and picking up the revolver, motioned Anne back into the other room. She shook her head resolutely and reached for the gun he had discarded. The door shivered before more ax blows. Clinch could not strike it fairly from his sheltered position, but a few more hacks would surely send it headlong into the cabin.

The top hinge parted, and the door fell in a few inches. Charlie heard an exclamation of satisfaction as Clinch attacked the remaining hinge. He braced himself for the rush to come when a quick shout came from the gap and a rifle spat rapidly.

Charlie's heart jumped. It was Lew!

A man outside swore in pain, and Charlie stepped up to the narrow window. Looking out into the dim light, he saw Lew charging straight up the valley, holding his gun before him and shooting from the hip. Such shooting was not so effective in terms of inflicting actual casualties, but the sight of that fearless rush demoralized the men clustered about the cabin door, and they turned and ran off into the valley.

Lew stumbled through the door. For once, Charlie lost control of his poised temper. "Where have you been?" he asked angrily.

Lew, satisfied that his charge had saved the day, decided to not discuss his desertion of post as sentry.

"I've been out in the hills watching Clinch organize his attack," he replied somewhat truthfully. "I persuaded one of his men to desert, and I followed up as fast as I could. You winged one back there near the gap, and I found him lying behind a rock nursing a creased shoulder. I relieved him of his gun before he knew I was there, and then I came tearing up here to save you. I creased another fellow before the door, but that's sure a rotten gun," he said, tossing the over-under casually into a corner.

Charlie did not buy all of this, of course, but his stern frown vanished at the cheeky casualness of Lew's half-cocked explanation. And Lew had certainly arrived in the nick of time.

"Help get this door back into place," was all he said. "We don't know when they'll be back."

They braced up the door and fastened it with heavy poles.

"Didn't they scamper when I came charging?" asked Lew, loath to let his daring escapade escape without the praise he craved, especially from the girl.

"They scampered all right," said Charlie, "but they scampered right into Big Thunder Valley, and we came here just to keep them out."

At that, Lew's bravado collapsed like a punctured tire. "I never thought of that. I'll bet a dollar they are crawling up the Devil's Chimney this second."

At this, Charlie looked serious and wrinkled his forehead.

Then Anne spoke, "They can do no harm there. I am sure there is nothing to steal, and as long as they are up in that cave, they can't hurt us down here."

"That's it!" cried Charlie. "We must bottle them up in the cave until help arrives, or until they find the upper entrance and escape on their own to the ridge above. Come on, Lew!"

They stepped outside quickly and then stalked cautiously through the early morning shadows. They found no trace of Clinch and his gang until they reached the cleft in the rock that led up into the Devil's Chimney. Charlie pulled Lew down to the ground as a man poked his head and the end of a gun out of the opening.

"They've put someone on guard," he whispered. "The rest are up in the cave, and I'll bet they are making the rock fly looking for those diamonds. Let's count up. There are only four of them left. This guard is probably the one you hit before the cabin door. I suppose he isn't hurt bad enough to keep him from taking a shot at us."

They could hear faint, muffled noises from far up in the cave.

"They're digging, all right," Lew said. "Well, we might as well crawl back down and fortify the cabin. We can't stop them from here."

Charlie considered the situation as they crouched at the base of the cliff.

"It looks like they still hold the upper hand, for now. That fellow at the entrance can stand us off indefinitely. The only thing is after the excitement of treasure hunting leaves them, they'll get an empty feeling, and that will drive them out, maybe even cause some dissension in the ranks. We can keep them bottled up, for now, but after dark, they can slip out anytime. I guess we had better retreat to the cabin and hold onto that."

Lew suddenly remembered the man Charlie had wounded back in the gap, the one whose rifle he had taken before he charged down and dispersed the party before the cabin door. They searched for him carefully among the rocks, but he had vanished. "I suppose he's had a stomachful and has gone back to some fallen-down shack back in the mountains," said Lew.

They entered the cabin, and Anne met them with questioning eyes. The strain was beginning to tell on her still-radiant face.

"Yes," said Lew, "they're up in the cave."

"Dad won't like that," she answered. "But I don't care. Both of you have done all you could, even if we've failed in guarding the valley."

"You've got a good head, Lew," said Charlie. "Now's the time to use it. We've got to pry those bums out of there without any more danger to ourselves than we can help. We mustn't get hurt, for Anne needs somebody to protect her. Think! What will it be?"

They thought silently while Anne began making an early breakfast. Suddenly, Lew spoke, "How far is it around to the ranch by the other trail? The road that Clinch drove his car over when he came in?"

"About forty miles," Anne told him. "Dad and I came over it when we first settled here, but that was so long ago I've forgotten the details."

Charlie looked questioning at him, and Lew explained, "I thought I might outflank them by coming over the mountain and then down through the cave. We'd have them surrounded, then."

Charlie shook his head. "It's too far. Besides, you don't know the trail and might wander around for a week before you found the upper mouth of the cave. No, we must do something from here, something more speedy than that!"

Lew turned to Anne. "Haven't you ever been away from here?"

"Just once," she answered slowly, dim memories bringing long-forgotten images before her eyes. "The year Mother died, Dad carried me up through the Devil's Chimney on his shoulder. I was eight years old.

"Mother had started to teach me, and Dad finished my education. He was a college man, before some trouble drove him into these mountains. He has never told me much about it. I have had to piece together words and parts of sentences to know that little bit."

They sat all morning, considering the situation. Then Anne sprang to her feet and stood before them. "Dad will be coming soon," she almost whispered, her face twisted with anxiety. "He will walk right into their hands when he starts down the cave. Clinch will be angry when he finds there are no diamonds, angry enough to do almost anything!"

Charlie stiffened as this new angle struck home. "She's right! Think, man," he commanded Lew.

Sometime after noon, Charlie walked cautiously to the entrance of the cave. The sounds were still audible, and he caught sunlight glinting from the rifle barrel of the man guarding the entrance. Lew met him outside the cabin on his return.

"The storm will break soon," Charlie said. "It won't take much longer for them to realize the diamonds are not there. I guess all we can do is wait and meet them in whatever way they attack."

Anne met them at the cabin door. "I'm afraid," she said slowly. "I don't know what it is, but my courage seems to be slipping. Please don't leave me alone again." She choked as a sob shook her slight body.

Lew pressed her hand between his own. "One of us will be before the door every hour of the day," he promised.

The cabin had been built right against the sheer face of a cliff that rose behind one log wall, straight up for hundreds of feet. Lew glanced up the dizzying height, and a rattle of loose stone sounded up on the summit. Then a handful of loose gravel came hurtling down, and striking the roof, bounced high into the air.

"Something or somebody is up there," he said in a low voice. They stepped back a few yards, motioning Anne under the shelter of the roof, and made their weapons ready for use.

A man's head rose slowly into view, silhouetted against the sky. He glanced at the group below, and drawing his hand back over his shoulder, threw something down towards them.

"Look out!" called Charlie sharply and raised his gun, but the man already had vanished.

Lew ran over and picked up the thrown object. It was a stone as large as his fist, and tightly tied to one side was a folded square of paper. "It's a message!" he cried. "Maybe it's from Anne's father."

That brought both Charlie and Anne over to his side, and they leaned over his shoulder as he spread out the paper. Then Anne read aloud:

"Dale Harmon walked down into the cave today. I have him, although I would rather have the diamonds and Anne. Tell her if she wants to save his life to come to the cave alone tonight. It will be too late after eight."

Anne broke into silent sobs.

"We've muddled everything," Charlie said bitterly.

For once Lew was quiet. He studied the note, and determination spread over his face. "We have until eight o'clock," was all he said.

Chapter 6 – Omega

Lew drew Charlie away from the cabin, out of Anne's hearing. "Listen," he began. "Clinch knows he has the upper hand as long as he holds the cave and Anne's father. We can't wait for them to come out and meet us fairly. They don't have to take such a chance. There is only one thing left. When a bear won't come out of his den and you want him badly enough, you have to go in after him. I'm going in the cave after Clinch."

He lifted his hand as Charlie began to protest. "As soon as the sun sets, I'll start. It will be dark in the valley, and that gives me at least two hours before the time Clinch has set for Anne to surrender herself at eight o'clock and save her father."

"It's not much of a plan," Charlie replied. "But I, too, believe it is our only hope, and I'm going in with you."

"No," Lew declared firmly. "Your place is here with Anne. You are the most level-headed man I've ever known, and she needs that sort of a protector. Besides, I got both of you into this mess in the first place. If I had stayed on the job last night, Clinch would still be outside where he belongs, and Harmon would be safe with us here.

"No, absolute silence will be needed for my success, and two make more noise than one. I've got to take them before they see me, and that starts with silencing the man on guard down at the opening. If I fail …"

He faltered a moment, then, but soon regained control of his voice.

"You stick with Anne. Get her away from these mountains. Don't let her sacrifice herself for her father. Stop her by force, if you must. Better by far to lose one than two."

When Charlie nodded assent, Lew went on with that same quiet determination. "But I won't fail," he continued. "I can't. Now let me lie out here in the shade and get a little rest. It's been a long night, and I want to think over my assault plan. Help Anne bear up the best you can."

Then he turned and walked over to a lone pine growing beside the river and threw himself down in its shadow.

Charlie watched him soberly for a moment and then turned into the cabin. After all, Lew was right. Yes, his plan was dangerous, not much of a plan at all, really. But Charlie could think of nothing better. He saw plainly that Lew had made up his mind, and with his stubborn determination, there was no use protesting. Nothing could change him. Lew had aged in the past few days, and his face was set like a man, no longer an impetuous youth.

Anne had retired to her own room, and Charlie could hear her sobbing softly, no doubt thinking about her father being held up in the cave by Clinch and his gang. What worried him most was the possibility of her insisting upon surrendering to Clinch.

"What use would such a sacrifice be?" Charlie asked himself. "Clinch could still kill her father, or hold them both, for his word is worthless."

He walked to the window and looked out. Lew still lay under the tree, on his back, staring straight up into the sky. Anne emerged from her room late in the afternoon and prepared supper. Charlie called to Lew, and a moment later, he entered the room.

They talked and even laughed as usual as they ate, but both men were watching Anne closely, looking for some sign of her intent. She offered no insight, however, and they both respected her silence and asked no questions.

At six o'clock, the sun set and darkness fell swiftly into the narrow valley. Lew arose, thrust Charlie's six-gun into a pocket, slipped a long hunting knife in his belt, and opened the door. Charlie accompanied him outside and would have walked farther but Lew motioned him back. They clasped hands silently—a firm, hard grip—and then Lew strode noiselessly off into the shadows.

Charlie stood watching, straining his ears to catch some sound that would tell of Lew's failure or success. A shout, perhaps, and a shot or two—this would mean he had failed. It seemed to Charlie he stood motionless for hours, eagerly listening and hoping he would hear nothing, but the only sound that reached his ear was the sullen lapping of Big Thunder among the rocks at his feet.

He turned as a noise came from the cabin, a thud as though a window had fallen. He assumed Anne was closing up the cabin against the gathering chill, and resumed his tense listening.

At last, he heaved a sigh of relief. Lew must either have won his way inside the cave or else found it impossible and turned back, in which case he could be expected soon. Charlie entered the cabin. He immediately noticed the total silence. "Anne!" he called into the back room.

There was no response. He stepped to the table, lit the kerosene lamp and looked anxiously about. The door of her room stood ajar, and Charlie opened it wide. There was no one there. Now genuinely alarmed, he ran out and called into the darkening valley. Only the echo of his own voice answered back from the rocky cliffs. Anne had left, and he knew where she was headed.

* * *

Lew strode swiftly towards the narrow cleft that formed the entrance of the Devil's Chimney. Fifty yards out, he stopped, removed his shoes, and crept on with stealthy care. He tested each footstep before leaning his weight forward. Soon, he was right before the door. The crucial time had come. Everything depended upon his silencing the sentry he expected to find on guard there.

Lew sank down flat on the ground and silently wormed around the curve in the cliff. He could see a faint glow, and there was an odor of tobacco in the air. A low shrub grew just at the corner, and Lew gratefully used this cover. He thrust his face into the leaves, peering into the opening.

A man sat six feet away, puffing on a pipe. A dim light shone down from the cave above. Lew drew back and considered his chances of executing a surprise attack. They looked rather small. The guard faced him, and his rifle lay across a knee, ready for instant use. But the man must be taken out, somehow, and with absolute silence. Lew also knew his chances for overcoming the man in a hand-to-hand struggle were good, better than even, but he doubted if he could prevent the man shouting and warning his companions back in the rock chamber of the cave. If he would only turn his back, just a second, it would give Lew the chance he needed.

An idea entered his head, and before he even had a chance to reflect upon it, Lew picked up a pebble, gathered himself together, peeped cautiously through the shrub, raised his arm, and tossed the stone accurately over the guard's head. It struck behind the man with a sharp rattle. Instinctively, the fellow turned, half-raising as he moved, and at the same instant, Lew sprang as lithe and agile as a mountain cat. He landed squarely behind the man. His hands shot out and grasped the man by the throat. Lew gripped as he had never gripped before. There was a strangled gasp, a brief struggle, and then the figure slumped. His resistance ended so quickly Lew was suspicious. He released one hand from the man's throat and reached with a lightning move for his gun. As he did, the other straightened and, with a sudden effort, cast away Lew's remaining hand and opened his mouth to shout. His weakening had been a clever ruse as Lew had suspected. But as he opened his mouth and gulped in the air necessary to call, Lew was ready. His gun descended with a crash full upon the man's forehead, and this time, he crumpled completely. There was no faking now. He was down and out.

Lew eased him down upon the ground and crouched, gun in hand. His heart pounded madly as he listened for some sign from above that would tell him the noise of their brief struggle had been heard. All remained quiet, and presently, Lew stooped over, tore strips from the unconscious man's shirt and securely tied and gagged him with it. He laid the rifle back in the shadows. It was too clumsy a weapon to carry up among the rocks.

Just as he straightened to resume his climb, a light step behind froze the blood in his heart, and he shrank back against the wall. Was he to be discovered after all? A dim figure approached swiftly yet silently from below. Could Charlie be following him against his express command?

No, Charlie was much heavier and taller. This figure flitted past lithely and vanished up into the shadows, but as it brushed by, he caught a glimpse of a pale face in the dim glow of light. Even in that brief moment, he recognized her. It was Anne.

He stepped forward to seize and stop her, but he was too late. She was gone, and his heart sank down to its lowest depths. Anne had gone to give herself up to save her father. She was trusting in the scoundrel Clinch to release him unharmed. What the devil had Charlie been doing?

Lew grimly followed with greater care and silence than before. He simply had to succeed with his desperate venture now. Clinch soon would have both father and girl in his power, and Lew knew he was their only hope. He crept forward toward the light, a cold purpose gradually replacing the hot rage that had possessed him.

Then he heard a sharp challenge above, an oath from Clinch, and a short cry from Anne. She had been discovered. He pictured Clinch's foul grasp upon the girl and ground his teeth but grimly held to his slow, careful pace.

"Father!" she cried out. And then a babble of voices filled his ears. He stepped more quickly. They were making too much noise up in the grotto chamber to hear his steps.

Now he could see the flaming pine knots that lighted the cavern, thrust into cracks in the rock. He crept on and wedged himself behind a dripping limestone column, peering around at the scene before him. Dale Harmon sat with his back to the wall, his feet roped together. His hands were free, but on either side squatted one of Clinch's men. Clinch himself stood before the girl, gloating over her surrender. Anne was looking him straight in the eye.

"Untie Dad," she commanded in a toneless voice. "I have come to you, and I expect you to keep your promise."

Clinch grinned at that. "Not so fast, my beauty! I only promised to spare his life if you came. I'd be a fool to turn him loose now. He must find the cache of diamonds for me, first.

"Hurry, old man!" he commanded. "Let's have the stones! Something is liable to happen to your girl if I don't get them, and quickly. Oh, I won't give her what you was going to get. I've something better in mind," and he leered evilly at Anne.

Harmon struggled vainly at the ropes that held him back. The men on either side jerked his hands down and whispered fiercely for him to be still. He turned an anguished face to Clinch.

"I'd give you every diamond in the world to save her, if I only had them!" he cried. "But my mine is only a prospect. I believe the diamonds are here, but under fifty feet of clay. Why don't you dig for them as I have dug for years? I will make you a full partner if you let Anne go."

Clinch openly laughed at that offer.

Then Harmon looked at his daughter. "Anne!" he reproached. "Why did you leave the cabin? You can't help me now, and you have only sacrificed yourself in vain!" Then he groaned and buried his face in his hands.

Anne stepped forward and faced Clinch again, the words falling cuttingly from her lips. "Do you mean you won't let Dad go, after I have done as you asked? You miserable, yellow hound!"

Clinch grinned again. "I haven't the heart to break up such a happy family," he jeered. "I ... " She struck him smartly across the mouth.

"Why, you ..." he started to leap toward her. Back in the shadow of the limestone pillar, Lew decided his moment had arrived. He drew the six-shooter, stepped from around the stone and drew a careful bead on Clinch. At his shot the fellow shrank back, gripping his side convulsively. Blood oozed from between his fingers, but he did not fall, and Lew realized his bullet had struck too far back. He took aim a second time.

The men beside Harmon started to their feet, but he turned the gun upon them, and they fell back. Lew again covered Clinch carefully, determined to end the struggle between them once and for all. He pulled the trigger with a grim satisfaction, but as the hammer fell something knocked the barrel aside and he felt a stunning blow in the small of his back. He turned, but not in time. A brawny arm encircled his throat, and he was jerked over a driving knee on his back. He fell paralyzed and numb from the wrench at his spine.

Looking up from the floor, he saw his assailant was the man Charlie had wounded in the gap, the man whose rifle he had seized in his charge upon the cabin and whom they believed had run off into the hills.

"Another fizzle!" he groaned and turned over on his side.

"That was pretty good, wasn't it, for a man with only one wing?" his captor bragged. "What'll I do with him now?"

"I'll settle with him in a minute," Clinch replied. "Here, help me with this!" and he motioned one of them to jerk off his coat and assist in stopping the bleeding of his wound.

"Now!" he resumed. "I'm tired of this fooling around. Here's where we make a clean sweep of things." He picked up his rifle, and swinging it by the barrel, stepped over to where Lew lay. As he passed Anne, she shrank against the wall. Something in her manner made him hesitate.

"I must pay you for that smack in the face," he said, and seizing her roughly, he forced up her protesting face and kissed her hard on the lips. The men laughed loudly as they turned to watch this play. Harmon jumped to his feet, jerked a flaming torch from the wall, and hobbled out into the passage.

They looked at him in surprise but did not seem alarmed until a motion from Clinch started one after him. Dale Harmon already had found what he sought. He reached the torch straight up with a cry of triumph, the flame touched something that hung from the ceiling, and a thin line of sputtering sparks shot upward.

"It's a fuse!" someone cried. "He's touched off the mine!"

Harmon stood, watching the spitting shower of fire, a wild look in his eyes. Up it shot and then vanished. The men looked at each other in fear. Harmon hobbled back to where Lew lay upon the rocks. They were all too confused and frightened to interfere with his movements.

"Quick!" he whispered. "Hug the wall!" He motioned Anne to join them.

A hollow, muffled boom came from above. Then came a grinding sound that roared with ever-increasing volume. The very sides of the cave trembled.

"It's the loose rock above!" gasped Lew. "He has touched off a planted charge at the arch of stone, and it is all pouring down upon us!"

He clung to the wall beside Anne and her father as a mighty avalanche of rock thundered down the cavern.

At Lew's words, Clinch's men turned with shrieks of terror and fled with wild leaps and jumps. Clinch hesitated, started back to get Anne, and then turned to run, but he was too late. The irresistible sweep of stone caught and hurled him against a wall. Lew's heart froze in fear as the rocks crashed past. Boulders brushed his clothes as they sped by with the velocity of a titan load of buckshot. He expected to be crushed, and he never ceased to wonder how they escaped destruction.

Then the storm of rock slackened, a few stragglers bounced and bounded past, and it was over. Lew struggled to his feet and stared out into the pitchy black that surrounded them. He fumbled in his shirt and found the pocket flashlight he always carried.

Anne had fainted, her white, drawn face gleaming with cameo clearness in the light. Her father crouched beside her, crying for her to awaken.

Lew gripped him by the shoulder, and pulling him erect, stooped over and gathered the girl in his arms. She stirred, breathed heavily and opened her eyes. They flooded with tears when she saw him bending over her. "You are safe?" she murmured. "And Dad?"

Her voice restored Harmon to his presence of mind.

"All safe!" he assured her.

Lew set the girl on her feet. "I wonder what has become of Clinch?" he asked and threw his light about the cavern. The reason for their escape from the avalanche was now apparent. Ahead, the passage turned slightly, and its curve had deflected the stream of rock away from the place where they had crouched in fear—the only safe place.

A groan sounded from down the passage. Lew turned and walked in its direction. He felt for his revolver, but it was missing. The knife still hung on his belt, and he drew that as he advanced. Lew had decided it didn't pay to take any more chances with Clinch.

Throwing the light before him, he saw a huddled form lying against a wall. It was Clinch. Leaning over, he saw the man's lower body horribly smashed, both legs broken and mangled.

Lew looked around for the rest of Clinch's gang, but all appeared to have made it out. Then a faint shout came from below, and he recognized it was Charlie's voice.

"Come up!" he called. Charlie exclaimed joyfully at Lew's voice and then climbed rapidly up the rocks.

They helped Harmon and Anne down to ground level and then went back for Clinch. It was a fearful task to carry a man in his condition, but somehow they managed to get him to the cabin. Harmon shook his head soberly as he looked down on the battered wreck.

"Both legs must be amputated," he said, "but we can't let the wretch die. He will be a cripple the rest of his life, and surely, that should satisfy the most exacting vengeance. I will find someone we can send for a doctor. It is a day's ride by horseback."

"Did you see Spad and the others?" Lew asked Charlie.

"I had just reached the door of the cave when they rushed out. I hollered at them to stop, but they never paid the least attention. I never saw men so frightened. And run? You'd think Old Nick himself was on their heels! They didn't even stop to untie the sentry you had trussed up so neatly. I let him loose myself when I saw things were coming to a close, and then helped him out into the valley with the toe of my boot."

"I guess we've finally seen the last of that bunch," Lew replied with a satisfied tone.

Two days passed. By then, Clinch had been carried away by what remained of his gang, moaning and cursing in the rude litter they constructed. In spite of his evil deeds and foul nature, both Lew and Charlie could not help but feel profoundly sorry for the maimed man.

The color slowly returned to Anne's cheeks, and she laughed and talked with none of the dread restraint that had clouded her the past week. Indeed, Lew and Charlie sometimes found it hard to believe the desperate deeds that had actually taken place in the little valley.

Charlie had a question for Harmon. "How did you happen to have dynamite loaded up under the loose rocks?"

Dale smiled, a bit sadly. "For some time, I had resolved to blow the charge and bury my workings if a stranger ever jumped the claim. I had Clinch in mind all the while. I was determined no other would benefit from my years of labor in that cave, and the privation my daughter had endured. I placed the powder and waterproof fuse over a year ago, and it was lucky for us that I did."

He was silent for a few minutes and then resumed.

"I never can repay you boys enough for what you have done. Maybe I have followed a rainbow trail, after all, but it has been the dream of my life to discover something that would enrich Anne and compensate her for the hardships she has suffered here for my sake. I will take her away, now. We have a little money, enough to start over in a place better suited to a girl of her age. The only way I can repay you is by giving you my claim to the valley. I believe you like to hunt and trap?"

He looked anxiously at them.

They both nodded vigorously.

"We will leave soon, but perhaps come back for a visit next spring? I will make over my homestead to you, too, and that includes the mouth of the valley, of course. I hope you can find enough of the things you like to repay you for your services."

They reassured him on that point.

"Maybe," hinted Lew, "something else, even more precious, will come my way, some day," and he glanced to the riverbank where Anne stood looking serenely down the valley of Big Thunder.

Anne and her father left the following morning. A mountaineer agreed to furnish the necessary saddle and pack ponies to take them back to Hawley's Ranch. Charlie never did find out what Lew said to Anne as he bid her goodbye, but from her flushed cheeks and moist eyes, he decided an accurate guess would come easily enough.

"It's going to be a long winter," said Lew as they stood watching the little party wind its way up into the outside range of hills, "even with all of this good trapping before us. Just think, old-timer, it's all ours. The fur pocket we've been dreaming about and never truly hoped to find. Can you beat that?"

Charlie shook his head. He was also thrilled at the prospects ahead. Everything had worked out splendidly.

"Fate was pretty good to us after all," he said. "You can send home that confession Clinch signed about his being the robber at Shand's jewelry store and clear up your name back home. Doesn't that tickle you?"

"I no longer care what they think," Lew replied scornfully. "All I can think about is trapping this valley—and Anne coming back in the spring!"

(The end)

Trap Lines on Big Thunder
Chapter 1 – Trails in the Snow

Lew dropped the box of traps he carried and grunted in relief. "How many miles is it now?" he inquired hopefully.

Charlie eased his own burden down and wiped his heated face. "We'll be at the top in a few minutes. I told you the best way was to haul this stuff around the long trail by wagon, but you were so all-fired anxious to get traps in the ground you insisted that we pack our stuff over Hog Back Trail."

A wide grin contradicted any impatience in his words. "We can't begin trapping, either, until we have more cold weather. I never saw such an impatient fellow. Come on, let's go!"

They shouldered their packs and toiled up the steep mountain toward the summit of the ridge. At the top, they rested again before they plunged down into the yawning top of the cave known as the Devil's Chimney, which led down into the valley of Big Thunder.

Up from the shadows of the valley came a long, wailing scream that sent shivers down their spines.

"What in God's name was that?" asked Lew in a whisper.

"Must be a cougar," answered his partner.

"Do they really scream like that?" asked Lew.

"Yes," Charlie replied. "I know some claim the big forest owls make a call that is often mistaken for a cougar, but no owl ever screamed like that. It was just the kind of unearthly scream I would expect from a lean deer-killer. We'll have to hunt him down to save the few deer left outside of the valley."

They climbed down through the winding cavern, past the pit where Dale Harmon had labored so many years in the hope of finding diamonds in the clay, now piled high and wedged full of the loose rock that formerly covered the top of the cave.

"I wonder if there is really anything down in that pit?" mused Lew. "Take a steam shovel to uncover it now."

"We haven't time to chase rainbows," grunted Charlie. "We're trappers, not miners. And if the fur is anything like it should be, we're going to be mighty busy this winter. We have to work fast, too. Fur will only be good six or eight weeks in this southern climate."

They squeezed out through the narrow seam in the rock at the bottom of the cave.

"This cave will have to be blocked up before we start to trap. If it isn't, we'll have to fight off the local trappers. They'll swarm in on us when they find there is such an easy back door to the valley. Since Harmon blew in the pile of rock that covered the top, the path is open to anybody."

"A couple of logs will fix that," said Charlie. "We've got our last load down, and we will do it in the morning."

Traps and supplies were piled high in the cabin, and when time permitted, they whittled stretcher boards from straight-split blocks of wood. At least one of them hunted every day, putting quail, rabbit and squirrel on the table.

They planned their operations systematically, first locating several dozen sets for fox and skunk then building cubbies and setting stakes to season and blend in with the surroundings. Charlie continually stressed the short trapping season, and they worked hard to prepare everything possible ahead of time.

A little cold weather was the only necessity, and this was beyond their control. The water animals were doubtless prime, for the Big Thunder River ran cold even in summer. But Lew and Charlie preferred to wait and take everything at the same time.

Charlie cast an eye searchingly up at the sky. "She's coming soon," he prophesied, and he was right. That night a norther swept down from the prairies, and they heard the gale whistle among the pines about their cabin and shriek down the open throat of the fireplace.

They shivered through three days of severe change. The squirrels they shot showed thicker fur, and a week later, when a light snow enveloped the valley, they decided it was time to begin setting steel.

They had planned two general lines, one leading down the valley on one side of the river and back up along the other, and another shorter line that ran entirely outside the valley. The homestead they had received from Dale Harmon lay partly outside the narrow gap through which Big Thunder entered the valley, and the adjoining land was uninhabited by any of the mountain folk. Here the fur was thin, for it had been steadily trapped over the years, yet Charlie believed an eight-mile line would pay off.

They did not care to trap their own valley too closely. When the outside traps failed to pay, they would pull them and concentrate along the river, but they were determined to stop trapping in time to leave enough animals to keep the valley stocked.

They drew lots for the lines. Lew was lucky and got the rich valley while Charlie grunted in disgust when he found he had drawn the outside country. This meant lots of walking for small returns. Charlie consoled himself with the thought that Lew would keep out of mischief if he stayed busy inside. But Charlie wasn't reckoning with Fate, who still had a few tricks up her sleeve, ready to spring when least expected.

Lew thought he could place about fifty traps a day in the valley, and Charlie thought about thirty would be his limit. The valley was a true fur pocket, rich in fox, coon, muskrat, mink, weasel, opossum, skunk, and at one spot Charlie found what he felt sure was an otter slide.

Several days before they started to trap, Charlie caught a skunk and a coon and hung their carcasses up in the sun. Then he drenched them with three bottles of trail scent, hitched them to a long wire, and got ready to drag them behind him while he staked out his line. He was determined to use everything he could to compensate for the thinly scattered sign he saw along his route.

Lew viewed the unsavory drag. "You'll have every dog in the mountains on your heels if you stink up the country with that mess," he said.

"Never mind, my boy," his partner answered. "I've got a hard row ahead, and I'm going to use every stunt I can think of. This is just a beginner. And I'll wager I make you hustle to get the same amount of fur every night."

They were both late in reaching the cabin after the first day setting traps. Charlie built a roaring fire of pine knots in both cookstove and fireplace while Lew skinned two rabbits he had shot. Lew was jubilant over the prospects he had found in the light, thin snow. "I'll have a load of stuff tomorrow night, old man. Wish I could get a pack horse to lug it all in."

"Don't skin your fur before you catch it," cautioned Charlie, who knew from experience that a single animal could leave a tremendous amount of sign in one busy night.

"There's a log lying along the river, bridging a still pool, and I know I'll have a mink there," Charlie went on, ignoring the caution. "He has used that log as a bridge every night this summer, and when he jumps off next time, he'll land slap in a number two trap."

They got an early start in the morning, and Charlie heard Lew whoop when he reached his first set trap, about 100 yards below the cabin.

Lew had caught a small coon at the edge of the river. The next three traps were empty, to his amazement, for Lew had expected to find them all full on this first day. Then he picked up a possum and a muskrat. Rats were a hard proposition, here, for the burrows led back into the bank, with entrances under one to three feet of icy water. Placing the traps was hard business, but Lew had taken an ordinary trap setter and spliced it out twice the original length. Even with this, Lew usually got splashed up when he arranged the final touches to stake and trap.

At the log bridge he looked eagerly for a mink. But when he examined the water's edge he saw where the wary animal had jumped neatly over his trap. Lew pulled another from his sack and set it exactly where the feet of the mink had landed in the half-frozen mud. Then he skillfully covered the pan with a wide leaf. He wore rubber gloves under his mittens to eliminate as much human scent as possible, and the mittens—new ones—had been smeared with fresh rabbit blood. These precautions would be especially important at fox sets along the base of the towering cliffs.

Lew knew he had a lot to learn about the wary reds and grays, and the more he learned about placing traps for them, the more he appreciated how limited his knowledge really was. The first set was empty, and he walked only close enough to see that the trap was still covered. The next had been sprung but lay bottom-side up. This, Lew knew, was a favorite trick of trap-wise fox— to spring the trap to show disdain of the trapper's clumsy skill. He carefully reset the trap still bottom-up. Now, if that cock-sure animal tried the same trick again, there was a possibility of catching him.

The next sets were empty, but finally, at the last fox trap, Lew found a half-grown red. He shot him neatly through the head with his .22 pistol. The next trap held a half-eaten rabbit, and leading away from the set was the strangest trail the trapper had ever seen. The footprints were sharp and clean in the light snow, but they were not of any animal Lew had ever caught. The paw marks were similar to those of a skunk, placed one before the other, but along with them were the plain marks of a dragging tail, a sharp line such as is made by a muskrat when it travels on the land.

Lew whistled in surprise. "Here's something to keep old Charlie guessing," he said to himself. "I'll bet the old boy will realize he don't know it all when I tell him about this."

At noon, Lew stopped to eat lunch and skin out part of his catch. He was steadily gathering a load that taxed his strength to pack across the rocky floor of the valley. He was disappointed in the catch of rats, but he and Charlie were more used to trapping rat houses than bank runs. Coon and possum were plentiful, and he added a skunk to his load with encouraging regularity.

Late in the evening, he staggered back to the cabin, tired but happy. Charlie was skinning a small pile of fur, and Lew dumped his load on the floor with a shout. "Eighteen pelts," he cried. "How's that for the first time around?"

"That's great!" answered his partner. "I've only got seven, not a big load but pretty good for my country. And—two of them are mink!" He drew out the long, slender animals for Lew to gaze upon.

"We'll clean up this season, for sure," said Lew, and he told how the sly mink had jumped from the log, neatly clearing his trap. "I'll get him, though. We should average twenty-five pelts a day, and with at least thirty days to trap, we're going to have a nice bale to ship."

Then he told Charlie about the strange trail he saw in the snow. Charlie straightened up from his task. "Feet like a skunk—tail dragging like a rat—

and the thing eats rabbits like a lynx or a fisher? You didn't find a cache of moonshine in the valley, did you?"

"Just be patient," Lew retorted. "I'll come dragging the critter in some evening. They can't dodge me long. I left the half-eaten rabbit and set two more traps around him. I may have him tomorrow."

But he didn't. A heavy sleet covered the valley when they started out the next morning, and both trappers found many traps frozen fast. Lew walked up to his log set for the big mink and found, to his disappointment, the animal had again used the natural bridge but had landed six inches to one side of the second trap. "I'll keep on setting here until I have the whole bank covered," he muttered to himself.

Up at the cliff he enjoyed better luck. The jutting rock had warded off the sleet, and the skunk and possum traps were well filled. But there were no foxes. Lew felt this keenly. He set a few more traps and hurried on to the half-eaten rabbit set. The bait had been cleaned up but the traps were frozen fast. A bear could have trod over them without any of the pans springing.

Lew rebaited the set and loosened his traps. He found Charlie a bit disgruntled that evening. "Nothing in my traps but two stray dogs!" he told Lew. "That scent drag brought them, all right. I haven't set a trap within three miles of a cabin."

Then he brightened and asked, "How about the freak animal—get him?"

Lew had to confess failure, and also his miss at the log mink set.

"I believe I saw bear tracks at the lower end of the valley today. I hope there's bear in here," he added on a positive note.

Two days passed and the fur catch remained small. Then the wind warmed in the night and both trappers looked for record returns. Conditions were exactly right for a heavy running of the night animals.

"If I don't get anything today, I might as well pull my traps," said Charlie. "Both of us will then make a killing in the valley."

But his luck turned, and he found three skunks and a possum. His keen eyes also noted a big decrease in tracks and sign, and he could not but believe that scanty as his catches had been, he without doubt had gathered in the bulk of the fur in the outside hills. He reset the traps carefully, hiding them well, and resolved to run the line every other day and help Lew out in between.

The warm wind alarmed Charlie. He knew the cold season had only started, but sometimes nature plays strange tricks in the Southern mountains, and a couple of warm weeks might start the fur prematurely on the downward grade in respect to quality.

He found a jubilant Lew at the cabin.

"I got him—the big mink at the log!" he cried, holding up a slim, long pelt that the practiced eye of his partner graded as extra large. It measured exactly thirty inches in length, and would stretch over four inches at the tail.

"I had seven traps set around the end of the log, and he simply had to land in one of them or else fly across," Lew boasted. "But I can't seem to catch the varmint that drags its tail."

Charlie accompanied him in the morning. Lew now had about two hundred traps out in the valley and along the banks of Big Thunder—a real man's line, and Charlie went with him the entire round to acquaint himself with every set.

Up under the cliff, Lew suddenly stopped. "Here, you old doubter, what do you make of this?" and he pointed to a small patch of snow under the shadow of the rock, across which ran a trail of round paw prints with a dragging line behind. Charlie bent over and studied the trail carefully. Then he straightened up. "If it wasn't for one thing, I could tell you exactly what it was."

"Sure," answered Lew. "Separate that tail mark from the feet, and any boy trapper could identify them both. It's the combination that has me guessing, too." The trail vanished out in the open where the snow had melted. Just ahead was a series of skunk sets placed before the crevices and cracks in the rock.

At the first they found the trap pulled in out of sight. Lew reached in his hand to remove it, but Charlie stopped him. "There's something on the other end," he cautioned, and Lew saw the chain twitch.

Charlie jerked up the stake and pulled steadily. "Watch out," he warned. "They are dangerous sometimes."

Lew looked up at that. Then the chain slackened, and a black object rushed out, spitting and snarling.

"It's a lynx cat," shouted Lew, as he jumped back and leveled his pistol.

"No," said Charlie, "but it's the next thing to one," and after the gun cracked, he held up a large, black feral cat—a common cat gone wild.

"Well," said Lew practically, "even house cats bring a price, although I'd a heap rather skin a skunk." He stuffed the dead cat in his sack. "It's better than those dogs you caught; you haven't anything to laugh about."

And then they discovered something that sent an uneasy feeling into their hearts and stopped both of their laughter.

"Don't you know better than to walk right up to a fox set?" asked Charlie, pointing to a footprint in the hard mud beside a number two trap.

"I should hope so," retorted Lew, and then he stopped short. "That isn't my track, Charlie," he said in a low voice. He placed his booted foot in the mark. It had been made by a shoe several sizes smaller.

They looked at each other in silence. Who had invaded their private fur pocket on Big Thunder? They had not been guarding the gap which was now the only entrance, but since the defeat of Clinch and his gang, the scattered settlers had shunned the valley carefully. All of them felt a wholesome fear of the trappers who had so bravely stood off the gang that came for Dale Harmon and his daughter.

They checked the rest of the line in silence, searching closely for more signs of the intruder.

"Look," said Lew, pointing to a coon set at the edge of the river.

"That trap has been reset. I never lay the spring at that angle. I always turn it the other way."

No other evidence of the interloper could they see, although they combed the valley carefully. They were lugging along a splendid catch, but neither felt any joy. Was their trapping here going to be a perpetual fight against trespassers as it had been up in the Northern bush country?

In the morning, Charlie started out for his own line, but he had only gone a few rods when he heard Lew shouting. "Come back," he called. "Somebody has robbed my trap below the cabin. He took something out, for there is fresh blood on the ground. It wasn't long ago, either. Let's go after him."

Charlie ran to him and examined the clumsily reset trap. A faint outline in the earth showed the same small shoe mark they had discovered yesterday.

"Let's go," said Charlie grimly, and they pressed forward at a fast pace. The shoe marks could not be followed, but the valley was narrow, and they visited each trap with sharp eyes for more sign. No other trap was disturbed, as far as the trappers could detect. All day long they searched the valley, gathering a splendid catch but no further sign of the intruder.

"That's funny," said Lew. "He only robbed the one trap, and surely a trap thief would grab off that mink or the big fox we caught back under the cliff. Suppose he heard us coming and hid in the rocks?"

Shaking his head, Charlie answered, "I don't know any more about it than you. He could hide out pretty snug in some of the shallow caves."

Charlie walked back and forth in the cabin that evening, deep in thought. Finally, he picked up his coat and gun and opened the door.

"I'm going to look around a little," he said as he vanished into the night.

Lew sat before the fire for an hour and then heard a step outside. Charlie burst in through the door. "Come on," he cried. "I think I've found him!"

They ran out together, and Charlie led the way down the valley toward the high cliffs. They passed the trap that had first been robbed, and Charlie turned up a narrow ravine and then stopped beside a tumbled mass of rock. He pointed up at the side of the mountain. "Look!"

There, in the pitchy gloom, Lew plainly saw a small point of light.

"It's his campfire. Shall we rush him now or wait until morning?"

"I'm not afraid, but I think it would be wiser to wait until daylight," was Charlie's answer.

"But how will we find the place tomorrow? There are dozens of cracks and caves in the rock."

Lew thought about a minute and then said, "That's easy."

This time he disappeared into the night but presently returned dragging a fallen sapling. "Here, line this up so it points at the fire; then, in the morning, we can sight along it like a gun barrel and see just which cave the fellow is hiding in. Then, if he is out, we can hide in there and wait for him to return."

"Good," said Charlie, and they rigged up the sapling, wedging it fast with loose stone until both were satisfied it pointed exactly at the twinkling point of light. Then they returned to the cabin.

At five o'clock, Charlie shook Lew awake. "Lets' start now. He's had time to slip out and rob a trap or two."

Picking up their guns, they stumbled out into the foggy half-light. They found the pointing tree and saw to their satisfaction that it was leveled exactly toward a small, narrow cave about twenty feet up and fifty yards ahead.

"Come on," said Charlie, and they climbed silently up over the boulders.

At the mouth of the cave they saw a small heap of dead ashes. Lew peered deeper inside and made out a sleeping form at the back of the cave.

"There he is," he whispered, and both trappers squeezed inside.

Chapter 2 – The Skagway Kid

Holding their rifles in readiness, Lew and Charlie watched the sleeping intruder. And then a bit of ash stirred up from the dead campfire outside the cave, lodged in Lew's nostril, and he sneezed loudly.

The figure under the blanket stirred and sat up with an exclamation. One hand darted under the blanket and dragged out a huge pistol, which he leveled on the trappers.

"Lord!" cried Lew. "He's only a kid."

A youthful face thickly planted with freckles and surmounted by a tumbled mop of hair glared at them.

"Youse right," he spoke in defiant tones. "I'se de Skagway Kid from Hell Roarin' Creek. What youse boys doin' in my cave?"

"Put the gun down, sonny," said Charlie after he had recovered from his surprise. "We won't hurt you. I don't think that field gun of yours would go off, but you might drop it and smash a toe." Lew chuckled at his partner's wit, but the Skagway Kid's face flushed in anger. He dragged back the hammer, and raising the gun high over his head, brought it down with a true Western flourish.

An ear-splitting report filled the narrow cave, and Charlie saw a splinter of rock go skipping down into the ravine below. The bullet had struck the side of the doorway.

"Won't go off?" derided the Skagway Kid from Hell Roaring Creek. "Let me tell youse some …" He stopped at the sound of a scurry from the extreme rear of the rock room. There was a rustle like that of dead leaves, and turning, he saw two shining eyes peering out of the gloom.

The Kid forgot the gun in his hand and sat petrified. Charlie walked back and kicked around in the corner. A dark, bushy object dashed out, nearly running over the boy as he crouched in fear. Then he shrieked loudly, and throwing away the heavy gun, fell over on his face.

Lew burst out in a hearty laugh. "Don't spring any more of that Hell Roarin' stuff on us, Kid. Honest now, isn't Kansas City as far West as you've ever been?"

The boy sat up with a crestfallen air. "What was it, a bear?"

"Just a half-grown coon," answered Charlie, "and he's as scared as you are. Better examine a cave before you camp in it. The next one might house a bear." He noticed the boy had spoken in normal language. In his terror he had forgotten the tough act of the Skagway Kid.

"Why didn't you get scared when we woke you?" asked Lew.

The boy hesitated a moment. "I've been watching you for two days now, and I knew you right away. You ain't the kind of men that hurt a fellow."

"What about that trap of ours you robbed yesterday?"

"Honest, I didn't take anything from your traps but two rabbits. I couldn't catch any myself, and I was getting awful hungry.

The trappers regarded him with compassion. He did have a hungry look on his pinched face. "I'll bet you could put away a man-sized breakfast right about now," said Lew. "How about a stack of corn cakes and bacon? Come on home with us."

The Skagway Kid rolled up his blankets, and picking up a tote sack holding his other meager belongings, followed them back to the cabin.

Over corn griddle cakes, they took turns questioning him. He was reluctant to talk, but finally, they learned that ill treatment had driven him from home. "Dad got to boozin' and cut up pretty rough with us kids after Ma died," he explained. "I read about the mountains down here, so I jumped a freight and rode as far as I could. I footed it the rest of the way. I worked at a ranch behind the mountains for a man named Hawley," here Lew and Charlie exchanged glances, "and one night I heard them talking about two trappers who were catching heaps of fur. I wanted to be a trapper, so I walked around the trail. Gosh, I thought I never would get here. I slipped past the cabin at night; I was afraid to show myself, for I got to thinking you might send me back home."

He shivered at that thought. "I'd rather do anything else than that. So I lived up in the rocks there and ate rabbits from your traps. You won't send me back, will you?" he pleaded.

"We'll have to think it over," said Charlie. And then he jumped to his feet. "Time to run the traps, Lew."

The Skagway Kid fairly leaped in excitement.

"Let's go," he cried. "I want you to show me how to be a real trapper, so I can go West and fight Indians."

"Hold on a minute, old-timer. The Indians have all been fought out the last fifty years. If you want to be a trapper that's all right, but you have to learn from the bottom up. Can you put yourself entirely under our instructions? A real trapper never whimpers, you know."

The boy nodded.

"Then," said Lew dryly, "you jump in and wash these dishes. Have the spuds peeled before we get home tonight and a pile of kindling cut for the morning. Also, keep up the fire and sweep out this shack. We'll make a trapper out of you, but you've to get the fundamentals first!"

The boy's face fell. Then he grinned. "I'm game," he said and started to take the dishes from the table.

That night, Charlie and Lew met a hundred yards from the cabin, both

The Adventures of Lew and Charlie

well loaded with fur. They dumped their loads, and squatting beside a rock, talked things over.

"What'll we do with the kid?" asked Lew. "I feel sorry for the little cuss. I know how my father whipped me every time I said I wanted to hunt and trap. Didn't it wring your heart when he told about saving up his pennies for two years to buy that cheap .22 rifle, and then the old man threw it in the stove the night he got home with it?"

Charlie nodded. "Looks like a bright little fellow. And honest, too. Remember he didn't touch any of the traps, only to get a couple of rabbits to eat. It must have been tough living up there in that crack in the rocks. He only had two worn-out blankets to sleep in."

"Well, if you feel like I do, we won't send him away," said Lew. "Suppose we instead show the poor kid the time of his life. It sure won't hurt him any to learn how to take care of himself in the timber and the mountains."

They stood up and started to the cabin. The fireplace shone out through the night with a blaze of light. When the door swung open they saw the Skagway Kid standing over the stove. A rush of warm air heavily loaded with the odor of frying bacon met the hungry trappers.

The Kid sprang to meet them. "Gosh, things smell good," said the always-hungry Lew. He cast a searching glance at the boy and noted with satisfaction that his face and hands had been scrubbed clean. That morning, when they found him in the cave, he had acquired rather a smoky appearance from living in such close quarters.

"Where's the fur?" he shouted. They spread the catch out on the floor for his inspection. Charlie named the different animals for him. "After supper, you can take your first lesson in skinning," he added.

The Skagway Kid fairly leaped in his excitement. "Say, but I'm glad to see you! It was awful lonesome today. Not as bad, though, as it was in the cave," he added. "Have you made up your mind about me?"

"Yep, old-timer," said Lew. "We're going to keep you for a time. Are you sure you didn't get into some scrape back home? Something they'll be looking for you about?"

The Skagway Kid shook his head. "I don't reckon they even missed me. The rest of the kids will have more to eat now."

He was just at the age when the quick mind and fingers of youth leap at any opportunity to learn. After watching Lew skin out a rat, he took the knife and surprised them with the speed and skill he displayed imitating the action.

"He's going to make a real trapper," said Charlie with a trace of pride in his voice. The boy flushed with pleasure at this praise.

Lew frowned warningly. "Mustn't let him get swelled up," he whispered.

"I don't think he is that kind," answered his partner.

The next evening, the Skagway Kid met them at the cabin door with a pale face.

"I heard something today. The awfulest scream," he said fearfully. "Sort of like a woman and yet it was different."

"It's the cougar!" cried Lew. "We heard him when we packed in the last load of traps. Remember, Charlie?"

"Was it in the valley?" asked Charlie.

"The noise came from outside," answered the boy. "Over there from those hills," he added pointing.

"Let's go after him tomorrow, or you can go, Charlie. I can't leave my traps right now."

Accordingly, next morning, Charlie made ready for the cougar hunt. He slung three powerful lion-size traps over his shoulder, and picking up the high-powered rifle, he turned to the boy. "Want to come, too?"

The Skagway Kid fairly flew for his coat and cap. They left the cabin and tramped obliquely away from the river over toward a low range of hills covered with rock and oak and an occasional towering pine. Charlie had skirted them when prospecting his trapline but found sign of fur animals so thin he never went back.

There was no snow upon the ground but a light layer of frost that covered everything like the nap of heavy velvet.

"Now, old-timer," Charlie began, "I'm going to be busy watching out for cougar sign and tracks. I've never been in these hills before, so you keep track of the way we go and turn so we won't get lost. I may have to depend upon you to find the way home tonight."

The Kid nodded. "I'se the Skagway Kid, boss trailer of Hell Roarin' ..." Then he broke off and added lamely, "I'll watch the best I can."

"That's better," approved Charlie. "I never did go much for that Hell Roarin' stuff, although I used to read those stories when I was your age."

Back and forth he weaved, covering each hill as thoroughly as he could, his keen eyes riveted upon the ground. He wished they had a good trailing hound—one trained to follow mountain cats. The hunt would then simply be a matter of locating a track and letting the dog trail until it treed the lion.

"Hello!" said the Kid presently. "This calf will have to watch out or the big cat will make a meal of him."

Charlie turned sharply. "Calf?" he asked, and stepping to the boy's side, he whistled. "Those are deer tracks, Kid. I don't see how I missed them. I'll say you've got sharp eyes. We'll follow them, if we can."

The tracks were faint in the frost and loose gravel, but after Charlie got started, he followed them at a fair rate of speed. For an hour they dodged about on the deer trail. And then, under a pine tree, one larger than the rest, they found where the deer tracks ended in a patch of blood-splotched earth and scattered brown hair.

"Keep back," warned Charlie. "The cougar's been here, and I want to read this sign before it's spoiled with footprints."

"He jumped down on the deer from the tree, didn't he?" asked the boy.

"Here's a good lesson in woodcraft for you," he answered. "Now, the average hunter might make the same guess you did. He would say the lion waited up in the tree until the deer came by. That flat limb stretching out over the bloodstains would make a dandy place for him to lie. There are no cat tracks near, only those the beast made when it dragged the slain deer over into the brush to eat it.

"But did the cat leap down from the tree? There is no regular trail under this tree, and a cougar might lie up there a week before he got a chance to kill and eat. And wouldn't a deer's instincts warn him of the danger overhead? Wouldn't he smell a lion so close to the ground? I guess we'll just look further before we jump to any conclusions.

"I've read a lot about these mountain lions, and the men who hunt them as a business say that ninety times out of a hundred, they stalk their meat and kill it from the ground. Let's circle around where the deer died.

"Here we are! See? The cougar came in quartering from the left. Look at the short steps he took until he got close. Here's where his toes dug in before he jumped. Now we'll go back to the deer's trail. I thought so. Just before the cat leaped, the deer started to run, but it was too late. There's the whole story laid out for the woodsman's eye to read. I don't pretend to be an expert, and there are fellows who could go over these signs and tell you more of the details, but I think we know enough for our business. We'll follow and see how far he dragged the deer."

They approached the brush carefully. Fifty yards in, they found the partly eaten carcass of a small doe.

"Lions waste a lot of good meat," grumbled Charlie. "They eat into the paunch and leave the quarters to spoil. But there's a good chance of this fellow coming back to finish this kill, for I know deer are thin in the mountains."

"Did you ever shoot a cougar?" asked the boy.

"No," answered Charlie, "and I never trapped one, either, but here is where we try."

He drew out the heavy traps and set them around the carcass. Then he stood up and viewed his work with a critical eye.

"I don't think the job is any too good, but same as you, lion trapping is something I've got to learn. Now, suppose we strike for home, old timer?"

The Skagway Kid turned around twice and then hesitated. "Which way is home?" he asked.

"Why, I thought you were keeping an eye on that," said Charlie in surprise. "I asked you to when we first started."

The boy dropped his eyes sheepishly. "I tried to but I lost track quite a ways back. When we struck the deer trail, I guess."

Charlie stopped short. "No use going on until we find the right direction. The sun is covered now, so we can't expect any help from it."

"Don't you know the way?" asked the boy.

"Why, I left it up to you," answered Charlie. "I kept my eyes on those deer tracks. Let's see. Which way did we start out this morning?"

The boy thought a moment. "When we left the cabin we were going east. The hills were in front of the sun; I remember it showed red behind them."

"Well, that's something," said Charlie. "These hills then lie southeast of the valley. What direction must we go to return?"

"Northwest," said the boy promptly. "Take out your compass and see which way that is."

"I'll be darned," said Charlie as he felt through his pockets. "I must have lost it."

This sounded like a genuine calamity to the boy. When he entered the valley he had followed a wagon trail and the river. "How do woodsmen tell direction in the mountains without the sun or compass?" he asked anxiously.

"I use three signs," answered Charlie. "Now cheer up, and don't get frightened. That's the first thing to remember when you are lost.

"The first sign is the moss growing on trees. Ever since I was your age, I have read how the moss grows heavier and thicker on the north or northeast sides of trees. This holds good, usually, but the woodsman has to always strike an average. See what I mean?

"We have moss on every tree trunk. But look and see where it is heaviest. And you find the heavy moss doesn't grow on the same side of all trees.

"Why not?" Charlie continued. "I'll show you. Moss grows best where there is the most moisture. The reason it should be heavier on the north side is that the sun doesn't strike there. The bark in the shade stays wet longer after a rain or snow, and the moss gets a start over that on the dry bark. But here is a tree that leans. Notice the moss is the thickest on the top. The top bark caught the most moisture. Here's another that's broken over into the brush. See, here's pretty heavy moss on the bottom. The brush held the moisture here. Come in the middle of this bunch of trees. You find the moss pretty even all the way around. Stick your knife in it.

"Now we'll go back to the trees around the edge. These are exposed all day long to the sun, and the north sides should hold the most moisture. I think we can safely trust this evidence. Yes, the moss is longer on the same side of the majority of these trees. But we'll go around on all sides and strike an average. You see, now, what I mean by averaging?

"A half-cocked woodsman might rush up to the first tree, and if the moss was heaviest on one side, he'd say that was north. Not so fast. Never forget to average. And watch out for conditions that might influence the sign you are weighing. A tree under the shade of a mountain? You couldn't trust the moss growing on it. The experienced trailer collects all of the evidence he can find and then sifts out special influences and strikes an average of what remains.

"Another pretty accurate sign is the rings in the wood and the bark of the tree. On big old trees, the bark is sometimes thickest on the north side and each ring—you know, the marks in the grain of the wood, each one of which means a year's growth—is usually thicker on the north than on the south. This is a pretty accurate sign. I'll chop a notch in three of the trees and we'll examine them."

Charlie attacked the wood vigorously with his belt axe, cutting a deep notch on opposite sides of each.

"Now look at them, Kid," he said.

The boy examined the rings of wood with interest. "Yes!" he cried. "They are wider on the same side, the side we have picked as being north."

"How about the bark?" asked Charlie. "Does it average with the rings?"

"No, it's uneven."

"We'll ignore the bark, then," said Charlie. "We have the average of two tests for direction, and we still have a third to consider. Let's start back in the direction we think is northwest and look for tall pine trees. You know the top branches, the very tips of pines, are supposed to turn towards the rising sun—to the east or a little south of east. There, I see one ahead. We'll look at it."

They examined the very tip of the tree carefully. The Skagway Kid's face fell in disappointment. "It points nearly the same way we're going," he said.

"So it does," answered Charlie. "Um-m-m. Let's see now. Something's wrong. I have it! This tree grows in an exposed place and every storm that sweeps down through the hills hits it full blast. The wind has turned it against its natural way of growth. It is the same way with pines growing in a narrow valley. The natural draft twists and turns them away from their tendency to point east. That's another thing you have to consider. We'll find another tree.

"Here we are. How about this one?"

The boy jumped gleefully. "This one's right," he shouted.

"We'll find still another, and if that bears out our direction we can push straight for home and be sure we are going right."

Hours later, they entered the gap of the valley. The Skagway Kid pushed out his chest with pride. "They can't lose us!" he boasted. And then a thought struck him. "Honest now, were you really lost?" he asked. "Or were you trying to teach me, so I'd know what to do if I got twisted?"

Charlie laughed. "We'll make a woodsman of you yet," he evaded.

As night fell they began to listen for the sound of Lew's whistle. It was time for him, now, and Charlie gradually grew anxious when he did not come. Charlie always felt a little worried when Lew was away from his own steadying influence, for his partner did have a habit of getting into trouble.

Finally, he decided to start out and search for his partner. The boy took a final look from the door as Charlie picked up his coat.

"I hear him now!" he cried. Charlie sat down in relief.

"He's got a load, I'm tellin' you," announced the Kid. "He can just stagger along. Why … what the deuce …"

Lew was now at the doorway. The Kid fell back in surprise.

"It's a … a … a fur shark!" he yelled.

Chapter 3 – The Mountain Killer

Lew laughed heartily as he dropped a long, sleek mass of dark fur on the cabin floor. "No, it's not a fur shark, Kid. Let me introduce you to Mr. Otter."

He sat down beside the fire. "Bring on the grub. Good Lord, but I'm tired. After I eat I'm going to tell you the strangest yarn you ever heard. I don't suppose you'll believe it; I wouldn't myself if it hadn't happened to me today. What do you think of this? I caught this big fellow in a coon trap about a mile down the river below the cabin."

"Hurry up and feed him, Kid," said Charlie. "I want to hear this. I know it'll be good. Lew never does things by halves, even telling a yarn."

"You can call me Jim," said the boy. "That was my name back home, before I started west to be a trapper."

"It's a good name for a trapper, too," answered Lew, and after he had consumed a prodigious amount of food he sat back in his chair and began to tell his adventure with the otter.

"I've been following that fellow most of the afternoon. Saw him the first time when I was at the lower end of the valley. I was sitting on a rock right at the top of the cascades that block up the valley at that end when I saw something floating down the current. I thought it might be a mink, for it was too big for a rat. I got my rifle ready and when it came nearer I saw it was the head of an otter. Remember those otter we saw up north, Charlie? Well, this fellow was coming down the rapids. I raised the gun and fired. He was coming too fast, and I didn't lead him enough, and I shot way behind him.

"When he saw me jump up to aim again he dived and turned back upstream before I had time to shoot. It made me mad to miss such an easy shot, for he was real close, so I followed him back up the river, keeping my eyes peeled for anything that looked like an otter. In about half an hour I saw him coming down again. I guess I got buck fever this time, for I shot too soon and the bullet plunked right before his nose. I was afraid he would get by me and go on down with the current. If he did this, of course, he was lost. The way he was swimming he could get down to the Gulf in a few hours.

"This shot turned him back again, and up he went like a streak of lightning. I began to realize that he was out to get by me and that he didn't want to stay up at this end of the valley. So I forgot about the rest of my traps and stayed on the bank of the river. What I was afraid of was he might come swimming down underwater so deep I couldn't see him, so I picked out a shallow place where I could see the bottom of the river and waited for him. I knew it would be longer this time, and sure enough it was.

"He came down just as I expected—underwater—and I plunked in two shots ahead of him and turned him back again. I just couldn't hold right to hit him, it seemed.

"I don't suppose you are believing this, but I turned him back three times and the fourth time I followed up a mile from the cabin. When he came that time, I cut loose with every shell I could. I was hoping all the time you would hear me shoot and come on down to help. This time he swam straight for the opposite bank to land. Believe me, I was worried then. Just let him take three jumps and he would be out of sight behind the rock.

"I steadied down for one last shot. Although I was already kissing that twenty-dollar pelt goodbye, I thought I might as well wait until he climbed out of the water, and that might give me a better shot.

"He hit the bank like a cannonball. In a flash he was on land, and I started to press the trigger, although I realized he was moving too fast for a hit. And then he stopped, just like putting on the brakes, and he jumped straight up in the air. I didn't stop to wonder why or what had happened. I just let fly and hit him square through the shoulders. He dropped, and I ran up to the ferry, crossed the river and ran back to where he lay."

Two hundred yards below the cabin, Dale Harmon had rigged up a small ferry across the river. A stout wire cable stretched from one bank to the opposite side and to it fastened with a running pulley was a small boat. By standing up in the boat, a man could grasp the overhead line and pull the boat from one side to the other. This was the only safe way to cross the treacherous mountain stream.

"Then I saw what checked him," Lew continued. "He had stepped plumb in one of my coon traps at the water's edge. It had a fair hold, too, enough to stop him until I could land that bullet. Just pure luck—fool's luck, I suppose you'll call it—for that trap only covered six inches of the hundred yards of bank he could have landed on."

Charlie glanced from Lew to the Skagway Kid who sat listening in open-mouthed wonder.

"We'll have to hand you first prize, Lew," he said sadly. "There's no use in me telling about the cougar and how we got lost today, is there, Jim?"

Lew didn't even hear the part about a cougar and protested hotly.

"It's all Gospel truth, every word of it. Remember how you kidded me about that feral cat? I suppose now you'll try to call this otter an overgrown mink. Here's the bullet hole. You can see he didn't die of old age."

In the morning, Charlie and Jim started for the outside line of traps and the set for the cougar beside the deer carcass. This was the first trip Jim had taken over a regular trapline and Charlie went slowly, explaining to him the reason why each set had been made, how the trap was concealed and covered and why bait was used or not used. When they found fur he showed how the animal was removed and how the trap was reset.

The catch was pretty slim, and Charlie decided to run the line once more and then pull the traps and take them down the valley. They did not catch enough to pay for the long tramp, but Charlie was glad he had an opportunity to show the boy about trapping in thin fur.

About noon they found a nice black skunk caught in a small cubby built of willow stakes beside a spring. Jim asked for the pocket pistol Charlie carried and for the chance to kill the animal and remove it from the trap. Charlie handed him the gun, and he approached the trap. The skunk sat facing them, and Jim walked quite close to make sure of his aim.

"Not too close," warned Charlie, and then he spoke sharply for he saw the animal slowly raise its tail and arch its spine. "Jump back!" he commanded, but Jim raised the pistol and took careful aim, instead.

"I'll get him before he can turn around," he answered confidently.

But the skunk did not have to turn. A thin green spray filled the air and the boy staggered back, gasping for air. His coat was saturated with the evil-smelling scent, but his face luckily had been spared.

Charlie choked back his laughter with difficulty. Jim stepped back out of range and fired. His aim was good, and the .22 bullet pierced the small head of the skunk. Then he turned to Charlie with a look of dismay.

"I thought they always had to turn around and shoot backwards," he explained. "What will I ever do with this coat?"

"Throw it away," advised Charlie. "You won't get cold going home and I have one in the cabin you can wear. It won't do any good to try to clean yours. Don't look so downhearted. It takes a couple of doses like that to make a real trapper. Sort of a baptismal rite or christening, I call it. Why, I know a trapper back home who was never satisfied or happy until he could tramp on a skunk and get scented up. He smelled natural that way, and his wife knew just when to set the coffeepot on the stove at night. She could smell him coming a quarter of a mile away."

Jim laughed a little, but for the rest of the tramp he remained silent. He walked behind Charlie, and when they approached the cougar traps he fell still farther back.

"Go easy now," cautioned Charlie. "I don't have any idea of catching that fellow the first night, but there's always a chance, and a trapped lion can be mighty dangerous. They can rip a dog to shreds with one sweep of their razor-edged claws. You don't want to get within reach, and if the traps are not touched, we don't want to leave any more man scent about."

At the clump of brush that hid the deer carcass Charlie halted. "I don't see anything, do you?"

"He's been here!" cried Jim pointing. And he had. The ground was torn up and two of the traps lay with their jaws sprung. The third was missing.

"He's pulled the trap loose and is dragging it. Oh, if we only had a good trailing hound now."

He examined the trail the beast had left. "We'll follow him as far as we can. The trap might catch on a rock or tree and hold him until we come up. We'll try it, anyway. Come on."

The trail was quite plain, and Charlie pressed forward rapidly to cover as much ground as possible before it grew too dark to follow. After the sun set, the lion tracks and the mark of the dragging trap would be invisible.

"I suppose he's five miles away. These fellows can cover a lot of rough ground in a day. I don't have much hope of …" he broke off as a low, throaty rumble, half-purr and half-growl, came from the brush before him, a sound that raised the hair along his scalp.

"Back, Jim!" he yelled, but before he could retreat himself, a dark, tawny form reared up from his very feet, its hard, topaz eyes gleaming with the fire of a savage, predatory lust.

Charlie instinctively thrust his rifle barrel forward, and the powerful jaws of the lion clamped down on the steel like a vise. In vain he tried to turn the muzzle so he could press it into the soft flank and fire, but two huge paws were reaching for his head and neck. Cougars draw in a man or dog with their teeth and front feet and then raise the powerful hind claws close to their own neck. Then the rear feet are suddenly straightened out, and razor-like claws rip to ribbons whatever is held in the deadly embrace.

Charlie felt the hot, fetid breath on his cheek and the forepaws fasten into his canvas hunting coat. The lion was handicapped with one foot fast in the trap, but Charlie could feel the free paw rise up and press against his chest. In a second he knew his abdomen would be in shreds. He knew the end was near, and a vivid panorama of his life swept before his eyes, ages of life, it seemed, were swept before his vision in that brief fraction of a second.

And then the boy who had stood terror-stricken at the sudden appearance of the foul beast rushed forward and with trembling hand pressed his huge pistol right against the slavering mouth and fired.

At the report of the gun, Charlie felt the claws at his breast pierce his clothing, and he shuddered. Then they relaxed, the grasp on his shoulders weakened, and with a desperate heave, he flung the beast from him. The lion slowly collapsed upon the ground and settled into a limp heap. Jim's bullet had struck it squarely in the brain. The boy stood shaking like an aspen, his face a chalky white in the twilight.

Charlie turned to him, and in a voice quivering with emotion, said: "I'll never make fun of that gun again, Jim. You and it saved my life. Another second and I would have been torn to shreds. Look," he stooped over the dead lion and pressed out the long, keen claws from one of the feet.

He felt himself carefully for wounds. His neck was scratched and there was a row of deep gashes in his chest where the beast had started to kick out the deadly hind foot when Jim's bullet ended its life. He drew a small first aid kit from an inner packet and carefully applied iodine to each cut.

Then he examined the dead beast. The trap chain had tangled about a dead oak stub and held it fast.

Charlie began to grow disgusted at his own carelessness. "That's what happens with poor trailing. Instead of looking ahead three or four yards, I kept my eyes right on my feet. If I had been attending to my business I'd have seen the cougar before I stumbled over it. The right way to follow a trail is to look ahead. At an angle, most tracks are easier seen than when you look down on them. And you don't run into tight places like I just did. I'll say it was a tight one. If I had been alone today, my trapping life would be over.

"I want to skin this fellow. It's a trophy I'll always keep. He must weigh close to two hundred pounds and be seven and a half feet long. We'll mount him this winter and make a swell rug out of his skin. I think I can do a rough job of skinning in this light."

He squatted beside the beast and plied his knife with skill and speed. "Have to leave the fine points about the eyes and mouth until later. Lew will be wondering what the deuce is keeping us."

It was a weary tramp home, and both sighed in relief when they sighted the narrow mountain gate to Big Thunder Valley. And then they saw a figure approaching through the gloom.

"I guess Lew couldn't stand it any longer," said Jim.

Charlie scrutinized the man coming towards them. "That isn't Lew," he said in a whisper. "Who the devil can it be?"

Then the figure caught sight of them. It stopped and then, turning to one side, walked swiftly out into the hills.

"Whoever it was, he didn't want to meet us face to face. I don't like the looks of this."

They found Lew in the cabin with a frown of worry between his eyes.

"I've had company," he said. "Did you meet that bird outside?"

"We did," said Charlie. "What did he want?"

"I couldn't make out exactly. He hinted around a lot and suggested some and I guess he's looking for trouble. He'll find it, too, if I see his shifty face in the valley again. Hello, how did you get scratched up?"

"Tell us what he said," commanded Charlie. "My story can wait."

"Well," Lew began, "I was getting supper when I heard a step outside. I thought it was you and then someone knocked at the door. This struck me as strange, for you never knock, so I stepped up and opened it, and there stood this hang-dog bimbo with a wide, oily smile on his face.

"He was real civil, saying as how we were sort of neighbors he thought he ought to pay a short visit. I had to ask him in, common politeness demanded that much. I noticed that he kept shifting his eyes all about the cabin as though he was looking for something or somebody.

"Finally, he said he had heard we had company, a boy who was staying with us. I didn't answer this, just grunted, I guess. But he went on to ask if we knew anything about the boy, where he came from and why he left home. Then he switched around to furs, regular old talking machine. Wanted to know if we were going to ship our catch and what we thought it might be worth."

"Then he hinted about the valley being too large for only two trappers. I believe the cuss wants to come in with us. Pretty fair nerve, I'll say."

"What did he look like?" broke in Jim. Both trappers glanced at him.

"Why, he's about forty-five years old, with a thin black mustache that sticks straight out on each side like rabbits ears. Thin and stooping man with a yellow complexion."

"I know him," cried the boy. "He was staying at Hawley's Ranch when I chored for them. He was the one that talked the most about you. About the valley here and the furs you were catching. One day, I told him I might come here to find you and he seemed eager to encourage me. He gave me that big pistol you laughed about."

"We won't laugh at that gun anymore, Lew," said Charlie earnestly. "It saved my life today—it and Jim's grit." And he told his partner of their fight with the trapped cougar.

At the end, Lew clapped the boy on the back. "I'll say you have pluck," he cried. "Lots of kids would have run off when that lion reared up on Charlie."

Then he turned to his partner. "I guess, old-timer, it's about time you stopped hinting around that I don't know how to take care of myself."

"But what about this fellow?" Charlie asked. "What does he want?"

"He wants his head busted!" answered Lew promptly. "There's an idea of some sort floating about between his ears. Does he know anything about you, Jim, something you've never told us?"

Jim shook his head vigorously. "If he thinks he's goin' to trap in here with us, he's cuckoo," he said.

"He isn't going back to the ranch tonight," said Charlie thoughtfully. "That's a two-day tramp. He must be lying out in the hills somewhere. I don't like that. I wish we had a big savage dog tied outside."

"There's all the fur in the log shed," reminded Lew. "Believe me, that would make quite a haul. Of course, we've got the door padlocked and it's a stout one, but one of us must stay home from now on."

"I'll stay," cried Jim. "That is if you trust me."

"We never doubt a trail partner," said Charlie quietly, and the boy flushed with pleasure at the words.

In the morning, Lew and Charlie started out to run the valley line. Lew had missed part of his line in following the otter, and they felt that both should make the trip. As they left they gave Jim strict instructions to stay close and let no one in the cabin.

"Use the shotgun on that bird if he comes snooping around today," was Lew's parting advice.

"That nine hundred dollars' worth of fur worries me a little. Jim is all right, I'm sure, but can he handle the job of watching it?"

"I don't look for trouble in the daytime," answered Charlie. "Usually, such fellows do their dirty work at night. No, I don't think Jim would take up with him or help rob us. He looks too clean about the eyes for that. If they were working together the fellow wouldn't have showed up last night. He could wait until we were both away and then clean up. Anyway, let's make this snappy."

"We'll split the line," said Lew. "If each one takes one side of the river we can get back by noon."

Shortly before noon, the trappers met back at this crossing. "You know," Lew confided to Charlie, "I've had a hunch all morning that everything wasn't all right back home. Let's creep up to the house as quietly as we can."

Keeping behind the tumbled rock, they approached the cabin with the wariness of Indian scouts. There were no windows in the back wall, and by keeping behind this, they were safe from discovery. Finally, they gained the shelter of the wall without seeing anyone and then they heard voices. They glanced at each other, and Lew held up his gun with a menacing gesture.

They crept noiselessly along the side of the building and stopped at the corner. They were only a few yards from the door and could easily distinguish the words of the speakers.

A strange voice said, "We'll try the fur shed first, Kid."

"That's him, the fellow who butted in last night," whispered Lew.

"Let me at the skunk."

But Charlie restrained him with a warning grasp. "Wait."

"I'm comin', Mister," answered Jim, and Charlie's heart sank. Was the boy a traitor after all?

Chapter 4 – Two-Legged Skunks

As they crouched in the shelter of the cabin wall, Charlie and Lew could only believe one thing. Jim, the boy who had descended upon Big Thunder Valley in the guise of the Skagway Kid from Hell Roaring Creek, and whom they had befriended and were teaching the art of trapping, had turned traitor and was helping the shifty-eyed stranger from Hawley's Ranch rob their well-filled fur house.

It was hard to believe, but they could not doubt the evidence of their ears, the import of the words just spoken. Lew grasped his gun and started forward, but froze in his tracks when he heard a crisp command.

"Hands up, you coyote!" They looked at each other wonderingly. What did that mean? A stream of curses broke from the man.

"You little devil! You double-crossed me!"

"Dry up," grated the triumphant voice of the boy. "Think I was going to let you rob them? Why, they've been better to me than my own dad. I'd let you kill me first. But you ain't got a chance."

In his excitement Jim now lapsed back into his role as the Skagway Kid. "Youse up against de Skagway Kid now, old-timer. I revels in the blood of sich stink-cats! Don't wiggle! If ole Calamity here goes off, thar won't be nothin' left of you but buttons, and they'll be a heap shot up."

A wide grin spread over Lew's face, and Charlie's heart climbed back into its normal position. The kid was all right, after all. Both trappers realized now how much they liked the boy, and this additional proof of his courage and honesty touched them. They walked around the corner of the cabin. The shifty-eyed stranger was backed up against the door. Before him stood Jim holding the menacing pistol leveled at his ribs and wearing a grin of triumph.

As they looked, the muzzle of the gun suddenly swept downward and a spurt of flame belched forth. A bullet plowed up the ground between the fellow's feet, and he leaped wildly into the air.

"Dance, you son-of-a-gun!" commanded Jim.

"Careful, Kid," warned Lew. "You might cripple the cuss, and then we'd have to pack him out of the valley."

Jim turned to them with mingled relief and surprise. "Gee, I'm glad you're home. This saddle-galled mesquite-louse came amblin' up here half an hour ago and wanted me to help him rob the fur house. I pretended like I would until I had a chance to get the drop on him, and then I stuck 'im up. What'll we do now? Scalp 'im?"

Lew considered this proposal gravely. "We really ought to, Kid," he answered. "I'd like to teach you the gentle art of lifting hair. Need practice myself, too. I must be getting rusty at it. Let's see if he's a subject to work on," and he walked over to the wondering stranger and jerked off his hat. A look of fear started to creep over the fellow's face.

Lew examined his hair critically. "'He ain't hardly worth it, Kid. Hair's too thin. Sort of mangy, too. I'd have to souse it in stock dip before you could wear it on your belt."

Charlie turned his head away to hide his laughter, but Jim stood watching Lew in wide-eyed interest. The stranger breathed with relief. He hadn't been able to decide whether Lew was joking or had been in real earnest.

"Now, you rotten thief," continued Lew grimly, "what have you got to say for yourself?"

The fellow sputtered. "He lied. He wanted to steal the furs all the time. Told me that's what he came here for, but when he heard you coming a few minutes ago he tried to turn it all on me."

Charlie laughed shortly. "That stuff won't wash. We only need to take one look to see who the rascal is. I've seen Jim in tight places before. I know he's good clear through."

Then his face hardened. "I'm going to give you some healthy advice. Get out of here quick, and stay out. This valley's plain dangerous for your sort."

The man hesitated then started walking swiftly away. But at the pile of rock that guarded the gap into Big Thunder Valley, he turned.

"Pet him up now, while you got the chance," he called derisively. "But I'm comin' back, and I'll bring the sheriff with me. He's a thief, he is. He stole that gun from me when he left the ranch," and firing this parting shot he ducked from sight. They heard him scamper up into the outside hills.

Jim shook with rage. "You liar!" he screamed after the fleeing man. "You gave this gun to me yourself." He turned to the trappers. "You don't believe I stole it, do you?" he asked anxiously.

"You bet we don't," reassured Lew. "He just said that because there wasn't anything else he could do to hurt us."

"What were you going to do with him?" asked Charlie. "Keep him cornered until we came?"

Jim nodded. "I was a little scared, but I was going to keep him standing there until dark if I had to." He continued, "Suppose he'll come back and bring the sheriff?"

"Not likely," said Charlie. "I don't know of any sheriff in these mountains, anyway. Don't worry, Jim. We'll stick by you. I think he was just bluffing."

Early in the morning, Charlie heard Lew hammering outside the cabin near the fur shed. He left the cook stove and went to investigate the reason for this daybreak activity. He found Lew and Jim had set two wolf traps before the fur house door. Lew was explaining to the boy just how large traps are covered with a ball of soft material under the pan which prevents smaller, lighter animals springing them. Charlie noted that the chains were securely spiked to the stout log doorjamb, and nothing short of a keen axe would unloosen the rings.

"What the dickens do you expect to catch here?" he asked.

Lew looked up with a grin. "From now on, partner, remember to step lightly when you come around the fur house. These traps are waiting for some two-legged skunk to come snooping around the skins. I notice there has been a sudden increase of this species. Jim and I reckoned we might wake up some morning and find a nice specimen waiting to be skinned and stretched. These traps won't break bones. They aren't strong enough for that, but they'll hold the varmint tight for a few hours."

Charlie laughed approvingly. "That's a good idea, but I'm afraid one of us will forget and walk into them. I don't wish you any bad luck, Lew, but if one of us should, I'm hoping it won't be Jim or me."

Lew was not put off. "I'll feel easier now when we are out on the lines," he said. "These traps are as good as any dog chained here. Better, in fact."

Charlie pulled the traps from his line outside of the valley that day. The catch was too meager to warrant spending any more time on it, and both trappers had agreed it was time to work the valley good and hard and gather in all the fur possible before warm weather came. There were only a few weeks left of trapping weather.

"I see plenty of sign, yet," said Charlie. "But there's no sense killing the goose that lays the golden egg. When the sign gets thin, we stop. If we handle things right, we may trap here the rest of our lives."

Charlie brought his traps home in two loads. It was after dark when he arrived with the last bunch, and he had a surprise for them.

"I ran slap into a nice bunch of wild turkey," he said, "not over a mile and a half from the cabin. And I didn't have anything but my .22 pistol. I didn't shoot, as I knew there wasn't any chance and it would only scare them. We'll hunt out there when we find time."

Jim was eager to go after the turkeys. He plied Charlie with countless questions about the place where he had found them, the habits of the birds and how to hunt them.

Charlie stayed at the cabin the next day and went over the skins, giving them a final scraping and removing from the boards those that were dry. They were running short of stretchers.

Lew had brought in a nice assortment. The skunk was not running so good, but he was catching more fox and muskrat.

At noon, Jim approached Charlie. "Could I take the gun out hunting?"

Charlie looked him over a moment before he replied.

"I don't like to let a boy take a gun out alone, but you are different. Any kid who has shot and killed a mountain lion and held up a fur thief must be pretty reliable. Sure, trot along. Be careful, though. Even old-timers have accidents, you know."

Night approached and finally Charlie straightened up from his work. "It must be later than I thought," he said. "Lew will be in soon, and I wonder what has become of Jim?"

A ringing whistle coming up from the valley told him his partner was home. He walked up to the gap and looked anxiously in all directions for Jim. "I hope he hasn't got into trouble," he muttered.

And then he saw something coming out of the dim haze at top speed. He watched eagerly and began to shout. "Lew! Hurry up here! Quick!"

Lew came on a run, but then stopped spellbound at the strangest sight he had ever seen. Racing swiftly towards the gap, came a big turkey gobbler with one wing trailing on the ground. Behind ran Jim brandishing his rifle in the air and whooping like an Indian. He was gaining steadily on the bird, and his face was red with exertion. They could hear him pull up and gasp fifty yards away.

Then he saw them standing in the shadows of the rock. "Grab him!" he shouted. Charlie sprang out in front of the turkey. It wheeled and darted back towards Jim, who spread out his arm to stop it. The gobbler swerved and dodged. It was reeling with fatigue and weakness from the wounded wing.

"He's getting away!" yelled Lew, dancing up and down in excitement. "If I only had a gun!"

But Jim leaped sideways with a desperate effort, and falling full upon the bird's back, clutched its neck with both hands. The gobbler thrashed and struck at him with its free wing and clawed desperately with both feet. But Jim held on with the determination of a football tackle.

Charlie ran up and struck the bird across the neck. It wilted into a limp heap. Jim stood and wiped his flushed face. He was shaking with excitement and fatigue.

"I chased him five miles," he gasped. Then he stooped to pick up the big turkey. He could just lift it from the ground, and when he held the feet as high as he could, its head still dragged.

"Ain't he a dandy?"

As they sat around the table, Jim told about his turkey hunt.

"I guess I tramped four miles without seeing a thing. When I came to that spring below the hill, where we caught a skunk last time we were out, I sat down to rest. The sun was feeling warm, and I laid down a minute, and I must have gone to sleep, for I woke up all of a sudden feeling stiff and froze, and there, drinking fifty yards down the stream, I saw three wild turkeys. I was so afraid I'd get buck fever I laid there a minute before I moved. Then I started to bring the gun around an inch at a time until I had it lined up on this big fellow.

"I was pressing the trigger when he straightened up with a sort of cluck, and I shot too quick. I only broke a wing. He jumped straight up in the air but couldn't fly. But when he lit, he was sure running. I saw the wing dragging, so I jumped after him, and boy, he took me on some race. He skimmed over the rock like an aeroplane, only hittin' the high places. I nearly gave it up, twice, but when I saw he was comin' straight for the cabin, I kept on. My lungs were about busted when I saw you standing there to head him off."

"Why didn't you stop and shoot him again?" asked Lew.

Jim looked at him blankly. "Gosh, I never once thought of the gun," he said. "All I could think of was running him down so I could get my hands on that slippery neck."

Charlie laughed heartily at that.

"He gave you quite a tussle before I whacked him over the neck. Well, Lew, I guess that beats your otter chase. We'll have to give Jim credit as the best hunter in camp. He sure stays after them until he gets them."

They hung the big bird up by the feet and dry picked him, the yellow skin shining bright in the firelight. Lew suddenly stopped with one hand full of feathers. "Say," he said, "do you fellows know what day after tomorrow is?"

They looked at him. Jim spoke, "It isn't …"

"Yep," cried Lew. "It's Christmas, and we've got the biggest turkey I ever saw. No meat market ever had a bigger one hanging up by his feet. Suppose old Santa will come to Big Thunder, Jim?"

The boy shook his head. "That's kid stuff. Anyway, he never found our house back in the city. Last Christmas, all us kids got was boiled pork, and believe me, we thought that was feedin' good."

Lew's jaw dropped at this. "Boiled pork for Christmas! How many of you were there?"

"There's two kids, both younger than me, Bob and Jenny. Gee, I wish they were down here to help us eat that turkey."

"I do, too," averred Lew heartily. "Anyway, I'm going to fill you up on real Christmas grub this year. How does roast turkey and fried rabbit saddles and baked coon and sweet potatoes and a few other trifles that the trapper finds along his path of duty sound?"

"Sounds like a dose of castor oil," put in Charlie. "I've got some sage put away that I found in the garden, and we'll crack hickory nuts and the oak chinkapins and stuff this bird with proper dressing."

Jim sat before the blazing fireplace so still and silent both trappers watched him curiously. Then he spoke slowly.

"Ma, she died just before Christmas. The doctor said she worked too hard. She was sewing shirts to get money to buy things for us kids, and then she died before she got a chance to give them to us Christmas Day. Gosh, it was cold then. We didn't have hardly no coal to burn."

He turned his face away to hide the tears. "It don't seem right for me to be here all warm with plenty to eat and not knowing how the kids at home are. How soon will I be old enough to earn some money trapping?"

Lew looked quickly at his partner, and reading assent in Charlie's face, spoke, "I reckon when you go home this spring you'll have something to take that'll help," and with this promise, Jim regained his enthusiasm at the approach of the coming holiday.

In the morning, Charlie announced that he had what might be called bad news. "Woodpile is low," he said, "and tonight is Christmas Eve. We must cut up a rick today."

Lew volunteered to wield the ax. Charlie looked at him doubtfully.

"There's something back of this. I never knew you to jump at a woodcutting job before. Not when you had traps to run."

"Truth is, I'm getting walked out," explained Lew. "You know I've been drilling up and down this valley pretty regularly. I'll appreciate a chance to stay here and work up some wood. Jim can help me."

Lew got out the double-bitted ax and carefully touched up the edges with a file. Then, with Jim at his heels, he set out looking for a dead tree that would burn easy, one not too far from the cabin to pack in.

"Trouble is," he explained, "all of the easy wood was cut years ago. What is left within toting distance is tough and twisted. Here's a black oak that'll make do."

He attacked the tree briskly, notching first one side and then the other. Jim watched with admiring eyes. "Gee, but you can handle an ax!"

Lew grinned and disclaimed all pretense of being an expert.

"You should see some of the mountaineers who live with an ax and a rifle in their hands. They can build a house with an ax. They swing it all day long and never change their breathing. They swing slowly but regularly, putting little more effort in striking than when they lift the blade. The trouble with most of us is we try to sink the blade too deep each time we hit."

He lopped off the branches and worked the trunk up into four-foot chunks, which he split or quartered while Jim piled them up in "pins" to dry out.

"We'll take a few hickory saplings for the fireplace. Hickory is the best green wood we have. Course, they burn better if they have a little time to dry out, but we cook with them lots of times the same day they are cut.

"Fact is, hickory is the best wood for the campfire, whether it is green or dry. Chestnut, dogwood, maple and oak are next. The poorest woods are the soft trees that grow along the riverbanks. Pine, sycamore, poplar, sassafras, ash, gum, tamarack and water oak are nearly unburnable when green."

"What does a fellow do when he wants to build a fire and the wood is all wet?" Jim asked.

"That shows a woodsman," said Lew. "You can always tell how good a man is by the time it takes him to start a fire in the rain or after a heavy shower. First thing he needs is wood that will burn, and then kindling of some kind to start it. Sometimes, a tree dies standing up from lightning or other cause. They make good, dry fuel. Split off a chunk by cutting two notches, one two feet higher than the other. This gives you dry wood.

"Sometimes, you can find dry wood in thick windfalls. Rick pine will burn in any weather, and is found in the form of old pine stumps or trunks that have rotted away, leaving the knots projecting from the hard center or heart."

He chuckled. "I remember one night Charlie and I found two hunters shivering in a small shelter tent. It had rained all day, and their wood was soaked. They had tried to burn green pine, and their matches were all used up. Finally, they gave it up and crawled in the tent, and lay there shaking with cold. The poor bums probably would have froze if we hadn't happened along.

"The funny part of it was I saw first thing an old pine stump standing right before the tent. Those fellows had firewood, the best in the world, right under their noses, and didn't know enough about wood to use it."

After dinner, Lew suggested to Jim that he go and meet Charlie, who would be coming up the trail in a few hours. "If he has a heavy bunch of fur, he'll be glad to see you coming to help lug it in. I'm going to split up some of this wood real fine for the cook stove."

Lew fell to work on the wood. As he worked, a shadow suddenly fell across the ground before him, and wheeling, he saw the muzzle of a big-bore revolver leveled at his face. Behind the gun stood a tall, lean mountaineer with drooping mustache and slouch hat.

"What the devil …" he began, but the man waved him back.

"Easy, son," he drawled; then, pushing back his coat, he exposed a large, glittering star. Lew's heart sank. This, then, was the sheriff, the revenge the fur thief from Hawley's Ranch had threatened. What a rotten Christmas for Jim.

"What do you want with me?" bluffed Lew, but in his heart he felt he already knew the answer.

"Warrant," said the sheriff briefly. "Warrant for Jim Doe, last name unknown. Charge of larceny. Where's he at?"

Chapter 5 – Secret Service

Lew halfway arose to his feet and then sat back. The sheriff looked at him keenly. "Haven't got no gun, have you?"

"We don't resist the law," answered Lew, wondering if their local reputation was as bad as that.

The mountain man, apparently satisfied, shoved his long revolver back in its holster. "Where's Jim Doe?" he repeated.

"Maybe I'm him," answered Lew. He was thinking desperately and trying to gain time. Somehow or other they had to get Jim out of this scrape.

"No," retorted the other. "He's a boy, 'bout thirteen years old. Don't get funny with me."

"Who swore out the warrant?" asked Lew. "Was it that shifty bird from the ranch?"

The man nodded. "Sam Phelps made the complaint."

"Let's see it!" demanded Lew.

"When I serve it," the sheriff answered. "It's all regular and sworn to."

"That fellow's a thief, himself," cried Lew angrily. "We caught him trying to steal from us. He's a pretty character to swear against a child. I know darn well he gave the gun to Jim. The boy isn't the sort to steal."

The sheriff regarded him stolidly. "Can't help that. Law's the law. I've got a warrant, and I aim to serve it. Where is he, I say?"

"Down in the valley helping my partner. They won't be back for maybe an hour. Where are you going to take Jim?"

"Back to the ranch. Hawley's a Justice. Mebbe one of you or both had better come along and back him up."

That had been Lew's idea all the time. One of them must go with Jim to be sure he got a square deal. But it looked mighty like the cards were stacked against him. Jim had the gun, and how could he prove the other had given it to him? It looked like the word of one against the other, and that of a local man would probably go. Could the boy get a fair trial in such a backwoods court? Lew could picture in his mind the trial as he thought it would be. It would be more or less a farce.

Then a bad intuition about the sheriff entered his heart. But the man had given him a tip. Perhaps he could learn more about the case, something that would help later.

"Who is this Phelps, anyway?" he asked. But the other closed his jaws like a steel trap. He shook his head. Evidently, he was through talking.

There was a shout behind them, and Jim came running from the cabin.

The sheriff started to meet him, and Jim stopped at the sight of the stranger.

"You'll have to come with me, sonny," he said in not unkind tones, and Jim drew back with a shadow of fear across his face.

"What for?" he asked. The man pointed to the star pinned to his rough hickory shirt, and reaching out, grasped the boy's arm.

Lew stepped forward. "Can't you at least wait until my partner comes back? Jim, where's Charlie?"

"He sent me on ahead. What does this man want with me, Lew?"

"It's that rascal from the ranch!" Lew said bitterly. "He's sworn out a warrant for you for stealing his gun!"

"But he gave it to me!" protested Jim.

"We're going to prove that, some way," said Lew. "Don't worry, old-timer. We'll stay by you."

"We're going now," interposed the sheriff. Then he turned to Lew. "If you're coming, better get a move on."

Lew hesitated. What should he do? He couldn't leave the cabin and the furs without telling Charlie what had happened and where they had gone. And he couldn't let Jim leave unprotected, either.

For a moment he entertained a rash impulse to close with the sheriff, jerk that gun from the holster and drive the man away. But luckily, his good sense came back in time to stop that. There was no use bucking the law. It would only be worse for Jim. Running off a thief you caught in your fur shed was a heap different than chasing the county sheriff away with his own gun. And then, as the man pulled Jim along the trail, a stranger stepped in.

He was a tall man, dressed in city clothes with white shirt and collar, and there was a confident bearing of authority in his demeanor.

He confronted the sheriff. "What's this?" he demanded crisply.

As Lew looked at this apparition, his jaw dropped. The sheriff's eyes were popping in astonishment, too, for the stranger had approached with cat-like tread. But the sheriff restrained his amazement and briefly explained.

Then the stranger stepped forward and smartly struck the sheriff's hand from Jim's arm. The man swore and reached for his gun, but the other held up a restraining hand.

"Stop!" he commanded. "So you're the sheriff of Cold Water County, are you? When did they have a new election? This morning?"

The man retreated a step and swore again, but this time Lew thought he could detect a tinge of doubt in his voice.

The confident stranger flipped back his coat and pointed to a small brown button on his vest. "Look here!" he commanded. "Know what that means? That's the United States Secret Service! I've got three men a hundred yards down the trail, so handle that gun easy. As it happens, my friend, I've just come from a conference with the sheriff of this county, and he looks a sight different from you!"

The look on the face of the bogus law man was so ludicrous Lew burst out in laughter. The fellow stood cringing for a second, and then with a wild leap, he sped down the rocky path. Jim's eyes were bulging from his head.

"How the devil did you ever think of that, Charlie?" Lew said. "I had to look twice myself before I recognized you in your dress clothes and that moustache! Was that why you sent Jim on ahead? Golly! That was better than a movie drama. I'll bet that bird is still running!"

Charlie grinned. "Jim didn't know exactly what I was up to. I merely told him to go ahead and not act surprised by anything that happened. I was afraid he would give me away, and I didn't know whether you could play up to my bluff or not."

"I hadn't any idea what was coming," confessed Lew, "but I did know enough to keep my mouth shut."

"We had just made the cabin when I heard somebody talking. I came up behind you, heard enough to know what was going on, and sneaked back to the cabin. For some reason the thing looked queer. I don't know what made me suspicious, but I decided our only chance was to run some kind of a bluff.

"I had to disguise myself some way, so I got out my good clothes, and believe me, I shook myself inside them in a hurry. I cut this sheik mustache from a strip of fox fur. Ain't it cute? Good thing I took you all by surprise. I don't believe the fellow had a chance to look me over closely."

"But what does it all mean?" asked Jim. "Why did he make us believe he was a real sheriff? What good would it do to take me away?"

"He's in with Phelps, our old friend from the ranch. They were playing the game together this time. What they really wanted was the furs. Maybe they thought Lew would offer to buy the sheriff off, but I think they wanted to get one or both of us away. If we went with you to see fair play, Phelps could cut back and rob the fur house and get away with it. Probably had a couple of pack horses tied up outside the valley."

Then he laughed heartily. "Did you see him stare at my Secret Service badge? Know what it was? My old National Rifle Association button."

"You're pretty good," Lew admitted. "That was a clever stunt. The only thing I could think of was to bust him over the head, but if he had turned out to be real, I'd have been in pretty deep."

"There was a chance of him being straight," said Charlie. "But when I first came up I thought I saw something shifty in his eyes. When I saw that, I played my bluff for all it was worth."

"Remember, Jim," warned Lew as they turned back to the cabin. "Brains always win over beef. Your Uncle Charlie had the right dope. Never bust a guy over the head when you can talk your way out of trouble."

"That reminds me," said Charlie. "What has become of the other fellow, Phelps? He must be around here somewhere. He might be snooping around the fur shed right now." And as in answer to his questioning, there came a wild yell from the direction of the cabin.

"He's caught in the traps!" Jim shouted and started down the path at top speed with both trappers close behind.

At the cabin door Charlie stopped. "I'm going in and change these clothes, first. I might want to play Secret Service man again someday."

Lew and Jim ran around to the fur house, and there, sure enough, they found the man Sam Phelps securely caught in one of the wolf traps.

He was hollering with fear, although the trap merely pinched him tight enough to hold against the desperate lunges he made to escape.

A stream of curses broke from him when he saw them. Then he stopped struggling and sank down on the ground with a groan.

"We caught our two-legged skunk!" Jim whooped.

Lew advanced cautiously a few paces and then halted. "I want to make sure before we get too close," he warned Jim. "Look him over carefully."

When Lew could see the man wasn't armed and wasn't going anywhere, he decided to have a little fun.

"Looks like there's a bit of coyote and hyena crossed in with the skunk. And it walks on two legs. Here comes Charlie. Maybe he'll know what sort of a varmint this is."

The man sputtered, choking with anger, both because they had caught him red-handed and also at the insulting nature of Lew's joking.

"Jump, boys," hollered Lew. "It's goin' to throw scent!"

"What's this?' asked Charlie innocently. "The critters must be getting thick when one walks right up to the cabin to get skinned."

"I bet the smell of the other skunks brought this one," put in Jim.

"Stop your joking and take this trap off my leg," Phelps demanded.

But Lew pretended not to hear. "Have we got a stretcher big enough to hold this hide, Charlie? It isn't very good quality, but we might as well skin it. I hate to ship trash, but we might get two bits for it."

"I'll set the sheriff on you," screamed Phelps. "I'll ..."

The trappers doubled up with laughter at that. "You ran that counterfeit sheriff off too soon," Lew gasped. "We could have chained them together."

At these words the thief fell into silence and began to regard them with eyes now tinged more with fear than anger.

Charlie turned to Jim. "Run and get my skinning knife. Bring my pistol, too. This skunk is too big to whack over the head with a club."

The boy looked doubtful at that, but Charlie winked one eye.

"What ... what ... you goin' to do with me?" the captive quavered. Lew and Charlie ignored his question.

"Reckon we better case it, or stretch it open?" asked Lew. "I'm sort of unfamiliar with this sort of skunk."

Jim came running back with Charlie's knife and gun. He took the blade and stepped forward. Now the captive's face blanched with genuine fear. Charlie appeared to be considering his options.

"I don't believe it's worth skinning, Lew. I hate to spoil a good bunch of fur with one junker. Suppose we knock this thing in the head and throw the carcass in the river?"

"You said it!" Lew assented eagerly. "Give me a club!"

Then the thief broke down, and crying for mercy, groveled at their feet, promising to do anything if they would just let him loose and not kill him. The cold-blooded talk of the trappers had broken down his nerve completely.

"What about the gun Jim stole from you?" asked Lew.

"He didn't steal it," the other groaned. "I gave it to him. Take this trap off my foot and I'll write it down and swear to it."

"That idea isn't half bad," put in Charlie. "Take him out of the trap, Lew. But watch him. Let the Skagway Kid hold that big gun on him until I come back." He hurried back to the cabin and presently returned with paper in hand.

"Here, you, listen to this." Then he read a detailed and full confession that concisely covered the conspiracy for making a thief out of the boy.

"Now sign this," he commanded. The crestfallen Phelps scrawled his signature and then started to limp off.

"I'm telling you the second time to stay out of here," warned Charlie. "Next time, we shoot without asking questions. We're too busy to be pestered by a buzzard like you."

When the fellow had vanished, the three entered the cabin.

"It's been a full day again," Lew sighed. "Nothing left to do but skin out twenty-odd pelts and put them on the boards. No wonder so many folks envy the trapper his life of ease."

Jim looked at him wonderingly. "Do things like this always happen to trappers? I thought all they done was set traps and shoot and hunt."

"You ain't half-educated in this trapping life, my boy," answered Lew. "These happenings today were just small pumpkins. He ought to have been up North with us, hadn't he, Charlie?"

Charlie assented. "Seems like we always run up against such skunks as this Phelps. He needed a good thrashing, but I can't lick a man when he's already down, and I think we've seen the last of him."

In the fall, the trappers had built a food cache up under the roof of the cabin and had piled it high with bags of flour, beans, rice, dried fruit and slabs of bacon. These provisions had been laboriously packed in from Hawley's Ranch. Charlie climbed down the pole ladder that led to this storeroom in the morning and confronted Lew, who was blowing the coals in the cook stove into a blaze. Jim was still asleep.

"We're going to run short of grub," Charlie said. "You know when we stocked up last fall we only counted on feeding two, and we bought just enough to carry us through. Now there's three of us, and we're making an awful hole in the stuff up there."

Lew looked up from the fire. "Man, this is no time to be talking about short rations. It's Christmas morning."

"Sure," answered Charlie, "but we've got to realize the condition of the grub supply just the same. That isn't all, either. You remember what a job it was to lug the grub in here, and we promised ourselves we would hunt steadily and use all the game we could get. Well, the last week we haven't hunted hardly any, and we've dug pretty deep in the beans and flour. From now on, we must live more on game; either that or pack in another load of grub from the ranch."

"And here I've been throwing away rabbits when I didn't need them for bait," Lew replied. "I've already eaten so many bunnies I dream about them in my sleep. But I'll bring them home now. Your Uncle Lew will pack a shotgun every day, too. I'd much rather eat rabbit than play burro packing more grub up over Hog Back Trail."

Lew ran the traps that day. He watched carefully for signs of game as he tramped through the valley. Usually, he would catch one or more rabbits in the skunk traps, and he thought it would be easy to gather up enough game each day to help stretch out the diminishing stores.

He found a rabbit in the first skunk set, but something had been there first and neatly eaten the animal, leaving only its legs and head. Lew examined the ground carefully and found the marauder was a lynx, a big one, too, if the tracks were any index to size.

There were two skunks and another half-eaten rabbit in the other traps. Lew muttered softly to himself. "If we didn't need the meat, I'd probably have caught a wagonload of rabbits today. We'll have to gather that lynx in pretty soon or he'll put a crimp in the easy game of the valley."

That evening, he returned empty-handed so far as anything eatable was concerned. "You'll have to send Jim out to drive in another turkey," he told Charlie. "That's the way with game; when a fellow actually needs it, there isn't a hair or feather in sight. I hunted all afternoon—hard, too—but blamed if I saw a thing. Everything seems to have holed or denned up out of reach."

"The sky has been looking queer all day," Charlie answered. "Sort of a copper haze over the clouds. If we were up North, I'd say we were in for a regular old blizzard with plenty of snow. But a little snow will help. We can find tracks and trails that should lead to a few square meals."

Lew looked at the pile of fur he had caught. "I suppose we might as well start in on those rats. I hate to do it on Christmas, but muskrat ain't bad. I draw the line at skunk and mink. We can eat the coon and possum, too, if we can just figure out where they all went.

"Is that turkey ready?" he added, brightening considerably.

"In a minute," answered Charlie. "I've got up as good a meal as I could. We can't start to diet on Christmas, so let's fill up tonight and not worry until tomorrow. I guess we can afford a little southern philosophy this one time. We'll be ahead of the game on kindling, you know, not having to cut kindling to cook breakfast."

Lew laughed at that. Then he told Charlie of the lynx which had eaten at least two rabbits from his traps.

"You better take a few big traps and make some sets for that fellow. We can't afford to feed another, what with the food running low."

When the big turkey, flanked with dressing, potatoes and gravy, reached the table, instead of digging in with his usual gusto, Lew only played with his food. Charlie looked at him keenly.

"Something's wrong, all right. Aren't you hungry? Usually I can't fill you up fast enough when you come in from the trail."

Lew pushed back his plate. "I feel sort of queer down in my stomach," he said. "Don't believe I'll eat any more," and then he arose to walk up by the fire.

Jim looked at Charlie, who shook his head in undisguised astonishment. Lew pulled off his boots. "I stepped in a hole today," he said. "That foot's been wet all day."

Charlie began to grow uneasy. "You aren't going to celebrate Christmas by getting sick, are you?" he asked.

Lew laughed shortly. "I'll be all right in the morning."

Lew turned in on his bunk, and Charlie sat back down at the table. But his own appetite was spoiled, too. He always dreaded sickness out in a trapping cabin. They had so far avoided any serious trouble, for they were young and strong and took excellent care of themselves.

"Is Lew going to get sick?" asked Jim in a whisper. Charlie shook his head. "I don't think so. He's just worn out with too much excitement and a hard day over the trapline.

But in his heart he knew better. When Lew turned down roast turkey on Christmas Day, things were serious.

"We've got lots of skunk oil," volunteered Jim hopefully.

Charlie sat up late that night. Every few minutes he walked in where Lew lay asleep. He was breathing heavily, and his head was hot to Charlie's touch. At times, he turned restlessly and muttered under his breath. Finally, Charlie turned in. He kept most of his clothes on and piled some slow-burning wood in the fireplace ready for any emergency.

He fell asleep instantly, and in his sleep, he dreamed of their car drive down into the Cold Water Mountains. He and Lew were spinning along merrily, loaded down with their camping truck. But suddenly, the motor started to emit strange noises. It was a low rumble that irritated his ears with the harshness of its tone.

It seemed they stopped the car but could not shut off the sound. It droned and rasped like a man puffing after tremendous exertion, and then Charlie awoke. The dream was such a reality he did not wonder when he heard the sound again. But then he realized that it was real, not a dream, and he sprang from his bed over to Lew's side.

Lew lay with eyes open, staring at the ceiling. His face was flushed, and his breath was coming with sharp, quick gasps that rasped through the half-light streaming into the room from the fireplace. His hands were clutched tightly across his chest, and Charlie's heart was gripped with the icy fingers of fear as he realized the truth. Lew was stricken with the dreaded specter that haunts all wilderness trappers — pneumonia!

Chapter 6 – The Big Snow

Only a moment did Charlie stand helplessly watching Lew gasp for breath as the cruel bands of pneumonia tightened across his lungs. As he always did in a crisis, he quickly grew calm and collected his wits by sheer strength of will. Getting rattled was the worst possible way to help his partner. He kindled a brisk fire, lit a long, homemade candle and sat down to think.

Just what did he know about pneumonia? He cudgeled his brains to remember everything he had ever heard or read about the disease. What rude remedies were at a wilderness trapper's command? The nearest doctor was forty miles away, and forty miles in the rough mountains meant a two-day tramp. In the morning, he would send Jim to the nearest neighbor, asking him to ride out for the medical man. It was the best he could do. Jim could hardly find his way in the dark, and for himself, his place was at Lew's side.

A quick turn for the worse might even end tragically.

"But what do people do for pneumonia?" Charlie thought desperately, yet calmly. Gradually, small bits of information began to rise up out of his memory. Pneumonia patients needed fresh air and yet they must be kept warm. Fresh air without chilling, that was it.

The open-throated fireplace gave excellent ventilation in the room, but Charlie arose and removed one of the windows. Then he covered the opening with a split burlap sack. This kept out wind and strong drafts yet gave the fireplace a better chance to clear the foul air and replace it with fresh.

He examined Lew.

"Cold, old-timer?" he asked.

Lew nodded his head. "Feet are cold," he said feebly.

Charlie would have traded the best mink pelt in the fur shed for a hot-water bottle just then, but he hunted around in the storeroom until he found a glass fruit jar. This he filled with hot water, and wrapping a flannel shirt about the glass, placed it at Lew's feet. He knew a laxative of some sort would be necessary. Pneumonia was a violent effort of the body to rid itself of accumulated poisons and waste matter. He was afraid to give the sick man anything drastic, so he mixed a half-teaspoonful of salt in a glass of hot water and bade Lew swallow it. Lew gulped the stuff down with a wry face.

"What the devil is the matter with me?" he asked. Charlie hesitated. Should he tell him the truth or pass it off as just a bad cold? He didn't want to worry and alarm Lew, but still, if he impressed upon him how serious the trouble was, Lew might at least take better care of himself.

"I think you're coming down with pneumonia," he said gravely, "but don't worry, we'll pull you through all right. Jim can start out in the morning and get one of the settlers to ride for the doctor. I'll stay here and do what I can. The main thing, for you, is to lie quiet and obey orders."

Charlie stepped to the door and looked out into the night for some sign of the rising sun. A snowflake struck him on the cheek. It was snowing easily and quietly. He hoped the fall would be short. Jim really didn't know the hills that well; he might have trouble finding his way in a snowstorm. He looked at his watch. It was only four o'clock. Lew might feel better in the morning. Sick folks were often worse at night.

He plied Lew with hot water, giving him glass after glass at regular intervals. It was the best treatment he could render with the limited resources at their mountain camp.

An hour later, he awakened Jim and told him the situation.

"Can you find one of the hill cabins?" Charlie asked.

Jim nodded. "I saw two the day we set the lion traps."

Charlie looked outside again. The wind had risen and the snow was falling faster; the flakes were large and fat and plumped down into his face with a sense of weight. It worried him. It looked as if Jim might have a hard time, but they simply had to get a doctor.

The wind increased, and they could hear it howling and shrieking through the mountain peaks high above the little valley. There were two inches of snow already. The long, narrow gash known as Big Thunder Valley was acting as a trough to catch the drifting snow below the storm. It was piling up, just as snow settles behind the protection of a hedge and drifts many times deeper than what falls on open ground.

Jim ate heartily and then began to button up his coat. Charlie took another look outside. The air was a gray mass of swirling snow. His heart sank as he realized he did not dare send the boy out in such weather. Jim would never find his way. It was too dangerous.

"You can't go," he finally told Jim.

Jim protested stoutly, but Charlie was firm.

"If you must do something," he said, "drag in that four-foot wood and pile it against the south wall of the cabin. At this rate, the snow will cover everything before night, and we must have plenty of wood."

Jim tugged and struggled through the snow, dragging the long split quarters to the cabin, where he stood them in a stack against the log wall. Charlie debated if he himself should start out for help, but a look at Lew's flushed face decided him. He might be delayed and not get back for days, and Lew was going to need constant care to pull through.

Jim came in stamping his feet, covered with snow. "Gosh," he said, "it's a foot deep already."

Charlie had never heard of such a heavy fall in the southern mountains. It must be an unusual storm, and a persistent one, too, for it still raged in the sky above. The wind did not strike the valley but passed over it as it glanced from the tall mountains that sheltered the river course. But the burden of snow still dropped silently down, and the heavy flakes soon covered the cabin and timber with a blanket of shocking thickness.

Charlie passed a restless night. He was up every hour, giving Lew hot water and replacing the hot jars at his feet. That was all he could do, just that and wait. Towards morning, Lew grew delirious and talked thickly in his sleep. Charlie fervently hoped the snow would cease when day broke, but in the morning it was falling as fast as ever.

Lew breathed in sharp gasps, and his face was burning hot. Things were getting desperate, with the storm outside and a shortage of food within. Charlie decided to use strenuous methods to relieve the fever which burned the patient with tormenting heat. There had been rough, unbleached sheets upon one of the beds in the cabin, and the trappers had removed these before spreading down their own camp blankets. Charlie found one and wrung it out in cold water. Then he wrapped it about the protesting Lew and then bundled him up in heavy blankets, with three hot-water jars at his feet and side.

Then he sat and watched him perspire. It was as good as a Turkish bath, and an hour later, when Charlie removed the wet pack, Lew breathed easier and soon dropped off to sleep.

Again, Charlie spent a sleepless night. He bundled himself up in his hunting coat and sat beside the bed. It was getting cold, the temperature dropping swiftly. Frost began to freeze over the remaining glass sash. Still, the snow drifted down from the speeding clouds above; the flakes were finer now, sharp and hard.

Lew awoke and began turning restlessly from side to side.

Charlie was dozing in his chair when shortly before morning he awoke with a start. Had someone cried aloud? He stood swaying as he rubbed the sleep from his heavy eyes. Lew was sitting upright in bed. ''My chest,'' he gasped. "It really hurts!"

Jim ran to him and watched Lew's suffering with tear-filled eyes. "I had it once when I was little," he said. "The doctor spread something all over my back and chest. He called it mud, but it was white and smelled good."

Charlie grasped at the suggestion. He must find something moist and heat retaining that he could apply to break up the congestion that was rapidly filling Lew's lungs. But what could it be? Jim was right, doctors did use a medicated clay, but they had none. Why hadn't they brought in such things last fall? Charlie determined he would never spend another winter trapping without a complete medical case.

Then he had an idea. He caught up his coat and hat, grasped the spade, and floundered out to the riverbank. He scooped off the snow and uncovered a patch of ground. It was only frozen lightly on the surface; the heavy blanket of snow had insulated it from the cold. He spaded furiously and soon found what he was seeking—a vein of soft, red clay.

He carried a bucketful into the cabin. It was the best he could find, and he felt sure it would help. He warmed it and mixed it until it was smooth and soft. Doctors used medicated clay—what could he put with this? He hesitated a moment and then got the bottle that Dale Harmon had left in the cabin and poured half a pint of whiskey over it. The stuff was nearly pure alcohol, for the mountain stills ran out a powerful brand of drink. He didn't know, wasn't sure if it would help. But it was penetrating and the best he could do.

He plastered the stuff half an inch thick over Lew's back and chest and then wrapped him up in three cotton shirts. Lew groaned and gasped alternately during the process. Jim watched with open eyes, amazed at Charlie's calm demeanor. "You're a regular M.D.," he said admiringly.

The snow fell until noon and then it stopped. When the pale, wintry sun broke through the clouds for a few minutes, Charlie opened the cabin door and looked around. The snow was banked high against the cabin, and when he stepped out he sank in up to his hips. It was three feet deep on the level.

"Man, what a storm," he breathed.

The valley lay like a narrow trough carved from solid white. The snow had drifted and hung curling over the mountain peaks in mammoth rolls, which would loosen when the sun began to thaw and avalanche into the valley below. But the weather was far from thawing. It was close to zero, Charlie guessed, astonishing for this southern climate. He could hear the timber snap and crack as sap-filled wood froze and burst from the shattering force of the frost.

Their traps were under three feet of snow; some probably held fur, but it would freeze and keep. They could dig it out later, but the big thing, now, was to get help for Lew.

Charlie took another step out towards the river and realized the futility of trying to walk even short distances without snowshoes. They had brought none of this winter gear. He laughed ironically. "Who'd ever thought we would need them down here?"

But snowshoes were needed, and he must contrive to make a pair or two at once. Yet even with snowshoes, Jim was too young to attempt a ten-mile tramp to the nearest cabin, and he dared not leave Lew—what could he do?

Just stick it out, he told himself.

　　　The Adventures of Lew and Charlie

He entered the cabin and closed the door softly. Jim was sitting beside the bed watching Lew's face. Charlie tiptoed over and gazed down. The patient was breathing easier than he had in two days, and Charlie thought his face less flushed. Maybe the clay poultice had been just right and was working already. He took up the axe and again floundered down the valley to a small clump of hickory saplings. He cut several of the straight young trees and dragged the butts back to the cabin.

Jim watched as he split the wood into quarters and shaved each splint to a half-round shape. Then he bent two of the strips in the form of an oval and lashed the ends together. He was making the simplest style of snowshoe — that known as the bear paw. Two cross stays were then lashed in the center of each shoe, with thongs of soaked green hide which would shrink when dry and tighten up with tremendous pressure.

Now the centers must be filled. Charlie, at first, thought he would use laces and then decided that a solid piece of hide laced about the edges of the frame would be stouter. He went to the fur shed and brought out a tough hide, shaved off the hairs with a keen knife, and put it to soak in a pail of water.

When the hide was soft, he cut it into chunks and laced two inside each bear-paw frame. He knew the hide and laces would tighten up and pull as taut as a drum head. He examined the finished product with a critical eye. It looked rough, and the green hickory was pretty heavy, but just the same, he felt sure it would bear his weight over the soft snow. He unraveled a length of rope and made strings to bind the shoes to his feet.

Jim was eager to try them at once with a short run over the snow, but Charlie set the shoes back away from the fire to dry slowly. "Tomorrow we'll see how they look," he said. "If they work, I'll make you a pair."

Lew was resting easier, and Charlie could not help thinking he was getting better. But just the same, he dreaded the approach of night. He realized he was completely exhausted himself. He had not slept much for three nights and had been going pretty steadily through the day. He decided to lie down and get a short sleep before night fell.

"You sit here and watch Lew," he directed the boy. "Wake me up at dark or if he wants anything special." He was asleep almost the moment his head touched the bed.

When he awoke, the sun was streaming in through the cabin window. He sat up and looked about in a daze. Hadn't night come, yet? Jim was still sitting beside the sick man. Charlie struggled to his feet and went to him. He noted with a sudden thrill that Lew breathed normally, and his face, though white and drawn, was free of the feverish strain.

"I didn't sleep long, did I?" Charlie whispered to Jim.

"Only since yesterday afternoon," was the answer, and Charlie quickly pulled out his watch. It was eight o'clock.

He had slept a solid stretch of sixteen hours. "Why didn't you wake me?" he said sternly. "I told you to wake me."

But Jim shook his head. "Wasn't no need. Lew slept fine, never turned once. I knew you needed the rest. I can't have two sick men on my hands.

"Say," he added, "I heard something jump on the roof of the cabin last night. About midnight, I guess. It landed with a thump, and then I heard a noise like something or somebody scratching around on the shingles. What do you suppose it was?"

"I'll look," said Charlie, and binding on the snowshoes, he opened the door. To his delight, he found they held him up splendidly, and after a couple of practice strides, he shuffled around to the rear of the cabin. The shoes were awkward, but they answered the purpose.

A tall pine grew close to the cabin, and several of its limbs reached out over the roof. In the snow Charlie saw the trail of a heavy, short body that had wallowed across the shingles. The soft snow had dropped back in the tracks so he could not tell what made them, but he was sure it was some animal, not a man. Whatever it was, it had reached the roof from the tree. He examined carefully about the bottom of the pine, but the snow was drifting, and any trail was filled level. He could not trace the direction from which the marauder had come or where it had gone.

He went back to the cabin and found Lew was awake.

"What the devil have you got plastered all over me?" he asked fretfully.

Charlie laughed. "I'll tell you when you're able to get up and shed it," he answered. "But you can gamble on this much. It pulled you through a bad case of pneumonia."

Charlie decided to walk the valley and look for game. Lew would soon be able to eat, and he would need something different from the beans and bacon he and Jim were eating. A brace of quail would be just the thing for a sick man to recuperate on.

The snow was still drifting lightly, and he found but a few tracks along the river. The animal life was still denned up or snowed under. A few rabbits had been out, and Charlie set several weak-springed traps and some wire snares along the trails. But for the most part, the deep snow was unbroken and unmarked. He knew there was no use trying to locate and dig out traps. When the wind stopped and the snow started to melt would be time for that. They needed food much worse than fur.

Lew was decidedly better that day. He had turned the crisis, but Charlie knew he would be weak for days and still need watching. The danger had not completely passed, for complications that would be as dangerous as pneumonia itself might set in.

Charlie spent the rest of the day rigging up snowshoes for Jim. He became more skilled with practice, and this pair turned out looking almost professional. Jim could not be restrained from venturing out, so he tied on Charlie's pair and started to get the knack of handling bear-paw frames in thick snow.

Charlie stood in the doorway and watched. Jim made it fine so long as he planted each foot carefully and slowly, but as soon as he started to shuffle forward at a half run, he caught one shoe on the other and pitched forward on his face. When he came in he was snow-covered from head to foot.

"I'm getting it," he laughed.

"Yes," answered Charlie. "By the time the snow melts you'll be a dandy."

Later, he would be mighty thankful the boy had learned to use the snow gear—and the rifle—as well as he had.

Lew continued to improve and began asking for food. Charlie put him off as long as he could. There really was nothing in camp fit to feed a sick man who had just weathered such a severe crisis. In the morning he was confident of finding rabbits in the snares. He would stew them up in broth for Lew.

Charlie started early in the morning. As he expected, the small game had been more active, and the snow was crisscrossed with trails. Mice had scampered over large areas, and several rabbits had pulled off regular frolics in the soft snow.

With a feeling of satisfaction, Charlie noted the tracks of two quail that had struggled through the snow. If he could just find them. He decided to follow the trail. He passed the traps he had set for rabbits—all were empty and unsprung. Then, ahead, he saw a bunch of fur in a snare. He hurried forward only to utter an exclamation of disappointment. The rabbit was half-eaten. Lynx tracks were all about. The big cat was going to put a crimp in any food snaring, he could see. He must run him down and add his hide to the stack of pelts in the fur shed.

Another snare held only the legs and head of a rabbit. This was more than aggravating, and Charlie swore aloud when, under a sheltering rock, he found ample evidence of another slaughter. Feathers and blood marked where the lynx had discovered the two quail under a sheltering rock. The animal had stalked and caught them before the birds could burst through the snow and fly to safety.

Charlie hunted desperately until the middle of the afternoon, and then was forced to admit himself beaten. He hated to go back empty-handed and face Lew's querulous demands for food. He was dead tired, too. Snowshoeing is something one must be hardened to by practice. Grimly, he turned back to the cabin. He might run into a rabbit—but he didn't.

Jim met him at the door. "What you got?" he asked anxiously. "Lew's been hollering for something to eat ever since you left."

Charlie shook his head. "We'll make him some tea and a little bean soup," he said. "It isn't what he ought to have, but tomorrow I'll get something."

Despite his natural ability to face privations, Charlie was becoming alarmed. He and Jim could make out for a couple of weeks, yet, but Lew's case was different. If he didn't find game tomorrow he would try to reach one of the cabins outside. He might be able to buy food more to a sick man's liking, although he realized the mountain folk were probably short themselves. This storm undoubtedly had caught them all by surprise and had cut into their supplies as much as it had their own.

In the night Charlie awoke suddenly. What had he heard? Was it the timber snapping outside? He lay and listened for half an hour but everything was quiet. Then sleep drugged his senses, and he dozed off.

He jumped out early in the morning. If he could get a quick start he might be back before Lew awoke and began to clamor for nourishment. Jim crawled out, and they quietly prepared a brief breakfast. Charlie emptied the flour can into the biscuit dough he was mixing. "Climb up in the loft and get me that last sack of flour," he whispered.

Jim sprang up the rough ladder. Suddenly, Charlie heard him cry out loudly. He ran to the ladder and saw Jim looking down at him with eyes wide. "There's a big hole in the roof!" he cried.

Charlie climbed into the loft and stared in horror at the sight before him. Something had clawed away the oak shingles that covered the roof. There was a two-foot hole gaping in the end. Holding the light above his head, he plainly saw the work of the marauder. Their scanty supply of food had been scattered all about. The flour sack was ripped to shreds, and the bacon was gone. Beans, rice and flour were mixed with dirt and lynx tracks.

Charlie held the light down to the tracks. "That blasted lynx!" he cried. "He's sure played havoc with our grub."

The food he had counted on tiding them over until the snow melted was ruined. A weak voice came up from the room below. "When the devil does a fellow eat around here, anyway?"

Charlie and Jim just looked at each other.

Chapter 7 – Big Game

It was one of Charlie's traits that any unforeseen emergency merely increased his determination and ability to cope with it. The raid of the lynx on their scant food supply was a stiff jolt, but he rallied quickly.

"Jim, you gather this mess up in anything you can find. The flour is spoiled, but you can pick out the beans and maybe sift out some of the rice. We've got to save every kernel we can. You can take the whole day to do it. Wonder if the beast dragged the bacon away with him?"

He thrust his head out through the hole in the roof. "Yes," he called. "There he went, dragging the meat in the snow."

He climbed down the ladder determined to follow the animal's trail. Gun in hand, he ran outside and examined the snow about the base of the tree. A puzzled frown gathered between his eyes when he saw no tracks, not a mark. How had the lynx got on the roof? Maybe it was still in the tree.

Charlie walked slowly around the trunk, scanning each limb for a flattened bunch of mottled gray and white, two eyes narrowed to slits and tufted ears pressed back against the fur. But he saw nothing.

"That's funny," he thought. "The cat must be either in the tree or in the cabin loft." He raised his voice. "Is he in there, Jim?"

There was a quick scramble and then Jim answered. "No, but you gave me a scare. I don't want to be in the same room with any wildcats, even if they are full of bacon."

Then the keen eye of Charlie solved the problem. A stiff limb halfway up the tree's height reached out to the cliff, and just above it he saw a narrow rift in the rock. That must be the cat's den. It had been living back of the cabin all the while, and growing bold with hunger, had torn up the loosely nailed shingles and got in the attic.

Charlie slung the rifle over his back and started to climb, but when he reached the limb he saw it was too weak to hold his weight. He descended and called Jim out. Showing him the cave in the rock he asked, "Can you skin up there and shoot him out?"

Jim was halfway up the trunk before Charlie had finished. He reached the limb and cautiously worked his way out to the end. Standing, he balanced himself against the rock and peered in the crevice.

"How deep is it?" called Charlie.

"Six or seven feet," was the answer.

Then Jim yelled in excitement. "I see him! He's in there eating the bacon!"

He raised the rifle. It was ticklish work balancing on the swaying limb, but his aim was true. When he fired Charlie heard a low snarl and then thrashing sounds from the rocks. Jim poked the gun in and out tumbled the lynx, spitting as it fell end over end and landed with a thump at Charlie's feet. It promptly affixed its teeth in his foot. Charlie jumped in surprise and kicked the dying animal off with his free foot.

"He'll weigh forty pounds," he cried in surprise. "We never saw such big cats up North. Any bacon left?" he asked Jim.

Jim poked around again. "He's chewed it all up."

Charlie carried the lynx inside. "We'll get plenty of rabbits now," he told Lew. "See what Jim knocked out of the rocks behind the cabin."

But Lew was only faintly interested. He did not realize how serious this loss of food had become. He called for grub, and Charlie tied on his snowshoes and left the cabin at the best speed he could manage. He must bring game home this time. All three were in danger of short rations, or no rations, unless he could shoot or trap something eatable.

Rabbits would tide them over a few days, but Charlie doubted if he could find enough to feed three men steadily. Bigger game was necessary. His rabbit sets were still empty. Something had tripped two snares but pulled free.

And then, when things were looking pretty bleak, Charlie stumbled on a deep plowing trail in the snow. His heart leaped. He knew well what had made those tracks. Deer! Two of them were plunging through the drifts ahead of him, searching for food the same as himself. Taking a new grip on his rifle, Charlie started out at a swinging gait. He would follow the trail a week if necessary, but he would get a deer.

The deer had wandered from side to side searching for food. The trail was looking fresher every minute, and when it finally turned up into a narrow ravine, Charlie breathed with hope. There was no way out of the draw except where he entered. He ran back across the opening. There was only one trail in or out. He had the deer bottled up.

Charlie slackened his gait, and holding the rifle in readiness, stalked carefully up the canyon. His keen eye scrutinized every object, every hump of snow and shadow behind the rocks and stunted timber. And then he saw them, two bucks huddled behind a thick cedar. They had winded him, their noses were pointed forward. He swung the gun up to fire swiftly yet with careful aim.

It was not easy shooting into the shadows, but he was an expert marksman and aimed at the head of the foremost animal. The rifle cracked loudly through the frost, and the deer plunged over on its side. The other bounded out in front of the cedar, pausing a moment while deciding which way to flee. Before it could leap again, Charlie's rifle cracked again, and the bullet caught it fairly behind the shoulders. It sank to the ground, kicking, and Charlie pumped another bullet into it. No use taking chances.

The first deer had fallen motionless. Charlie walked to them and cut the throat of the last one shot. Then he stooped over the other and thrust the keen blade into its neck. But at the touch of steel the animal suddenly leaped up, kicking the gun from his other hand. Charlie stepped back in amazement, realizing in that furiously brief moment that his bullet had hit too high, at the base of the horns, and only stunned the buck. As it lunged at him he dropped the knife and seized an antler in each hand, hanging on for dear life.

His blade had penetrated the jugular vein, and he knew it would only be a few minutes before the animal would bleed to death. If he could hold on until then, it would drop over. It lunged and reared, jerking him from side to side, but he held on grimly with a grip of iron. Then the jerking stopped, and the deer collapsed at his feet.

Charlie wiped the sweat from his brow. "That was a close call," he said aloud. "That buck tried his best to jab his horns in me, and I haven't time to waste bulldoggin' deer."

He dressed both, slung one up in the top of the cedar tree, and tying the feet of the other together, slung it over his back and started for home. The going was hard, with the extra weight of the venison pushing him deeper in the snow. Before the cabin door he shouted and Jim swung it open. When he saw the deer across Charlie's shoulders he danced with glee.

In a few minutes the odor of cooking venison filled the room, a smell that made their mouths water. Lew sniffed eagerly. "It's bad enough to be sick, let alone starved," he said. "Bring on about a gallon of that soup. Did the lynx eat the onions, too?"

Charlie waited only long enough to start the venison cooking and then, despite his fatigue and hunger, started back for the other deer. He could not take any chance with losing the meat. Another lynx might climb the cedar and spoil a big share of it during the day. The smell of the kill would bring any half-starved predatory beast from miles around.

Charlie swung down over his old trail with a light heart. That was sure a lucky stroke, two deer just when they needed meat so badly. He was tired and hungry himself, but in an hour he would be back at the cabin with a two weeks' supply of food. When he entered the narrow valley he stopped in surprise. Here was a strange, fresh trail cutting in from downriver, following the tracks he made when he packed out his first load.

Charlie stooped over and examined the marks. What were they? The soft snow had tumbled back into the footprints and he couldn't decide. But they resembled dog tracks. Perhaps some of the half-starved curs from the hills outside were hunting in the valley.

But when he approached the cedar where his deer hung he knew. Three dark shapes squatted on their haunches in the snow, eager snouts pointing up towards the tantalizing smell of fresh blood and warm meat. Wolves!

The big, gaunt wolves of the swamplands, driven to the hills by hunger, caught sight of Charlie as he paused, turned towards him, trotted up a few yards, then stopped and watched with hungry, crafty eyes.

Charlie unconsciously raised his arm and then remembered. In his hurry to get back he had left the rifle at the cabin. His only weapons were the .22 pistol in his belt and his knife. He jerked out the pistol and looked at the magazine. It held a single cartridge.

The wolves were sniffing warily. Then the leader, a rangy black fellow as strong and powerful as a mastiff, took a step forward. He acted exactly as if he were testing the man, trying him out to see how far he could advance.

Charlie began to feel shaky in the pit of his stomach. Why the deuce hadn't he brought the rifle? If those half-famished brutes decided to attack, it might be a serious scrape. He could kill one with the pistol, perhaps another with the knife, but they were three to one and could spring from three sides.

He mustn't let them sense his fear. He wasn't really afraid, either, for he had never known a wolf to attack a man. But these beasts were desperate with hunger, they looked starved enough to try anything. He took a step towards them and yelled loudly. They swerved back, trotting to one side, but then stopped and watched him again. It looked as if they wouldn't be scared away. The smell of deer meat was whetting their courage along with their appetites.

Charlie decided to back off, run to the cabin and bring back the rifle; then he could finish them and add their skins to the pile in the fur shed. Three wolf hides would be pretty good wages for any trapper.

He backed slowly away, a step at a time, keeping his eyes on the brutes. His actions puzzled them for a moment, and they moved nervously about in the snow. Then one started out to the side and around him. Charlie began to really worry then. The wolves were trying to cut off his retreat. He knew he had to decide what to do immediately. He didn't dare let them get any closer. The closer they came, the more confidence they would have.

He decided to fight his way through to the tree and climb it for safety. Then he would have time to think the matter over. Holding his pistol in one hand and his knife in the other, Charlie suddenly charged forward, yelling as he came. He rushed straight at the wolves and they slunk back out of his way. He ran as swiftly as he could, between them, past the brutes for the cedar.

As soon as his back was to them, they came with a rush straight for him, snarling with eagerness. Charlie made a desperate jump, reached the tree and started to scramble up the trunk. He kicked desperately to loosen the snowshoes;

they were clogging his efforts. The wolves came with a rush. One shoe fell off, and holding the other foot straight out behind him he climbed into the lower limbs. The foremost wolf snapped its teeth about his ankle and he reached down with the knife and slashed the brute across the snout. It fell back with a yelp, and Charlie, breathing heavily, swung up into the center of the tree. His foot ached badly, and he realized the wolf's teeth must have pierced his boot and tore the flesh.

Perched in the cedar, Charlie took stock of his situation. Now that he was safe, things took on a humorous slant. He had read tales of being treed by wolves but had never imagined that he would be in that predicament. He had one shell in the pistol; he could possibly kill one of the wolves. But he doubted that would drive the others away. They were evidently too hungry to fear death. In fact, it was probably death either way for them, by bullet or starvation, and they seemed to have lost all fear of man.

Then Charlie felt his own gnawing hunger and realized he had left the cabin without any breakfast. Lew and Jim were probably gulping down huge quantities of venison stew at this very minute. He was ravenously hungry, nearly as hungry as the snarling brutes below.

"Well," he said to himself with his natural philosophy, "I've often heard that raw meat is more nutritious than cooked. Let's see how much truth there is in that hearsay." He climbed up and cut a chunk from the deer's saddle.

He chewed it slowly. The meat was still warm, and it brought back both strength and courage. There would be plenty of snow clinging to the cedar branches when he got thirsty, although Charlie knew eating more than a little snow would be a bad idea. He could hold out longer than the wolves below. They might slink away when they realized there was no chance of their eating. Or he could throw the deer down if that became absolutely necessary. They probably would leave after they had gorged themselves.

But Charlie decided this would be a last resort. He and his companions needed this meat. They probably wouldn't get another shot at deer this season.

The sun climbed to its noontime height. Charlie began to wonder what Lew and Jim were thinking. Would Lew send the boy out to search for him? He had told them where he shot the deer. Lew couldn't come, but the boy might. Then a new fear entered his heart. Jim might come unarmed. If he did, those wolves would make short work of the boy. They would drag him down and rip out his throat in a second.

Charlie climbed higher and watched up the canyon. He glanced down at the wolves. One suddenly cocked its ears and pointed its snout down the ravine. Someone was coming. Charlie started to shout a warning, but before he could cry out, a rifle cracked and one of the beasts rolled over in the snow, snapping at its side. The others pounced upon the stricken wolf and tore it to pieces.

Charlie climbed higher until he reached the swaying tip of the tree. There, standing upon a big rock a hundred yards away, stood Jim with the rifle still at his shoulder. He was aiming again. Another report, but a clean miss this time. The remaining wolves never lifted their noses from their horrid feast.

Deciding it was time for him to lend a hand, he climbed down as near to the ground as he could and shot one of the remaining wolves expertly in the back of its skull. Another shot from Jim, and the last brute started to limp off.

Charlie shouted, "Hurry up, you've got them now. Watch out for that one you winged."

A minute later, Jim's rifle spoke again, and the wolves were all accounted for. Charlie unslung the deer carcass and climbed down to the ground. Jim approached with a grin spread over his face.

"Looks like you were sent down here to get us out of scrapes," Charlie told him. "When did you start worrying about me?"

"Just now. Lew kept asking why you didn't show up. Finally, I said I'd hunt you up. Lew got mighty cautious then, made me bring the rifle, and I had to promise him I'd come carefully and watch for trouble every step. He kept saying you must be in trouble, and I mustn't get caught in the same pinch. So I promised I'd come like a regular Indian scout, and when I saw the wolves under the tree I knew right away what had happened."

"I was worried you'd rush in and let them pull you down," said Charlie.

"What Lew said kept me from that," answered Jim. "I figured it out and climbed up on the rock where I was safe. I had plenty of cartridges, and I could keep shooting until I got them all. I shot pretty good, didn't I?"

"I'll say," said Charlie. "Your marksmanship was worthy of any hombre from Hell Roarin' Creek. Now," he resumed, "we'll skin these fellows before we go back."

He stripped off the hides, bundled them up for Jim to carry, and slung the deer over his own shoulders. "Did you give Lew anything to eat before you left?" he asked.

Jim grinned. "He was chewing the hind leg when I left. That ought to last until we get back."

"I hope he leaves a little," Charlie said with a smile, and then he told Jim of his own lunch of raw venison.

"Gosh," complained Jim, "you get all the fun. First, you shoot two deer; then wolves tree you and you have to eat raw meat to keep alive."

"I didn't hog all the fun on purpose," said Charlie dryly. "Anytime you want to double for me in such stunts you're welcome. I'm aching for a stretch of peaceful, quiet life about now."

That night brought a change in the weather. One of those lightning changes typical of the southern mountains struck the valley in the shape of a warm southeast wind. The snow began to soften and settle. In the morning, Lew was so much better Charlie decided to start out over the traplines and uncover what traps he could.

It was hard work. He dug and scraped away snow that was packing into a dense, wet blanket. Everything looked so strange and unfamiliar he had trouble locating many sets. He collected three skunks by the cliff. Although they had been dead several days, Charlie thought the fur still good. By nightfall, he had dug up over forty traps. Rabbits were running again, and he reset and baited.

Before he reached the cabin, a warm rain came pelting down from the sky. This would probably end their trapping, Charlie thought. The land animals would get "springy," and the fur soon would start to slip. They would have a week more to catch water animals, but the coon would quickly go bad, too.

All night the rain beat against the roof of the cabin. The snow sank to a mere skim of white, and Big Thunder came booming down its channel. The heavy influx of snow water was swelling the river.

"There goes our water sets," said Charlie as he stood in the cabin door the next morning watching the angry flood sweep down through the valley. "I'll bet traps and all are washed away."

"We'll be lucky if the river doesn't flood us out," answered Lew. "How the devil can that narrow channel handle all this snow?"

"We're twenty feet above the water now," said Charlie. "I think that's safe enough. But it won't do any harm to watch."

"What will we do if the river does come up to the cabin?" asked Jim.

"Crawl up the Devil's Chimney," answered Lew promptly.

Charlie donned a slicker and started down the valley. He walked close to the river looking for trap stakes, but they were under many feet of raging brown water. Huge chunks of ice and snow came hurtling down the river.

By the time he returned, the river was already over the bank by the cabin. He decided they had better prepare for the worst. He went to the fur shed, and with Jim's help, baled and tied the pelts in bundles. These must be moved in case of a flood. Nothing else was so valuable. Charlie was conservative, but he was sure they had nearly two thousand dollars' worth of prime fur.

After supper, Charlie kept walking outside to examine the river. But it hadn't swelled much, so he finally sat down before the fireplace and dozed off. Jim and Lew were sound asleep.

Charlie awoke with a start. What was that noise outside? He looked outside and then sprang back with a shout. "Quick! The water is ten feet from the cabin! The valley is flooding, and we must run for the cave!"

Chapter 8 – Wild Water

At Charlie's alarm, Jim and Lew sprang to their feet. They could hear through the open door the swirling water sucking at the ground around the cabin, a sound of sinister power that terrified them with a sense of their own helplessness. Lew clutched the wall, and Jim ran to the door to see.

"We must run for the cave. It's the only chance," Charlie said

"But the furs," protested Lew. "They will be lost, washed away! We can't leave them."

"There's no time," Charlie said. "We can just get away ourselves."

Then Jim turned back inside the cabin with a white face. "Too late," he cried. "The water is five feet deep between us and the cave!"

Charlie shot out the door towards the Devil's Chimney, the long rock cavern whose upper end reached to the plateau high above Big Thunder Valley.

Jim was right. Just below the cabin, he found a flow of dirty brown water over fifty yards wide. The river had backed up into a low draw and cut them off from the cave.

He could swim it, but what about Jim? It would be fatal to expose a weakened Lew to that icy flood. No, their only chance, now, was to flee through the gap into the outside hills. As he ran back he saw the water was nearer the cabin, lapping closer and closer to the log walls. Then he had a new thought — the ground was lowest at the gap. Harmon had built the cabin on the highest knoll of ground.

He ran only a few yards before the swelling flood again blocked his path. Big Thunder, swollen with rain and snow water, was breaking all bounds. They were hemmed in on all sides, trapped by the rising tide.

Jim met him in the door. "Where can we go? What can we do?" he implored in frightened tones. "Can we climb on the roof?"

Charlie shook his head. Stout as the cabin was, it would never stand the irresistible pull and sweep of the river as it poured down through the valley.

But they must do something — and do it quick!

"The lynx cave," he shouted, "behind the cabin! That'll hold us!"

He bundled Lew into a heavy coat and pushed him out the door. "Climb man! Climb the big pine!" Lew wobbled out to the tree. He was very weak, but Jim boosted, and slowly he dragged his body into the lower branches. Charlie was searching swiftly through the cabin for a rope. At last he found a stout coil, and giving it to Jim, commanded him to climb to the cave.

Jim scurried up and let down a free end of the rope. Lew grasped it, and with Charlie pushing and holding him from behind, he finally made the ledge and lay panting beside the boy.

"Look sharp now!" cried Charlie. "I'm going to send up the furs. Pull like crazy when I tell you."

He was working like a beaver, tossing the bales of hides out of the shed and tying them to the end of the rope. Jim pulled vigorously, but the water was lapping at Charlie's boots before the last one was hoisted away. He splashed back to the cabin. There was a foot of water inside now, and he grabbed the blankets from the beds and brought them out for Jim to haul up.

He made one more trip inside the cabin. He swiftly tossed everything loose up into the loft. It might be the water would stop climbing before it reached that level. And for a while yet, they could scramble down from the cave onto the roof, and by opening the hole the lynx had made, pull up more supplies. Then he picked up the two saddles of venison and ran back. They might be marooned in the cliff for a week, and Charlie didn't relish the thought of going hungry again.

Panting, he hauled himself up beside the others. There was barely room for them, furs and all, but Jim spread down the bundles of fur as smoothly as he could. "They'll make soft beds," he grinned. Already Jim had recovered his youthful confidence. Charlie's ability and quick action in the emergency had restored his courage.

They looked out down the valley. A pale moon lighted the wide flood of foam-crested water. In the center, its light was reflected in glimmering waves. But out at the sides, the cliffs were engulfed in dark shadow.

"It looks like one big lake," said Lew.

Charlie looked at him keenly. "You aren't cold, are you? Feel any worse for your climb?"

Lew said he didn't feel any worse.

"I'm awful tired, though. Guess I'll turn in," and lying down on the piles of fur, he drew a blanket over him. Presently, he spoke, "How's a fellow going to have pleasant dreams with all this skunk odor floating about?"

The scent was pretty thick in the shallow cave.

"A bed of hides is better than a flooded cabin," Jim replied.

"Well, old-timer," Charlie asked with a smile, "how do you like the trapping life now?"

Jim nodded with satisfaction, pleased to be included as an old-timer.

"I always wanted to live like Robinson Crusoe," he replied. "Maybe we can build a boat and float down through the valley." And then he hesitated. "The water … won't … can't … get clear up here, can it?"

Charlie was thinking this same thing, but he hastened to reassure the boy. "There's a mighty big hole at the lower end of the valley for this water to pour out of. Say, I'd like to be there now and see it rush over the cascades."

But in his mind he was wondering when the zenith of the rise would come. He had heard of flash floods in mountain valleys climbing to unbelievable heights, forty and fifty feet, and then sweeping down to wipe out entire villages. He feared to estimate how high Big Thunder might come.

"Get some sleep," he ordered Jim. "I'm going to watch. I'll wake you if there's any danger."

He surveyed the cliff above them. An man might climb up, hanging with his very teeth, and the let down a rope for his companions. Well, he sincerely hoped it wouldn't come to that.

He sat in the door of the crevice all night watching the flood rise below while his companions slept. It was creeping more slowly; he judged there was four feet of water in the cabin. Huge chunks of frozen snow came plunging down at intervals and smacked with heavy impact against the walls, but the sturdy structure withstood the battering.

And then the pale light of the moon faded into the twilight of morning, and a red sun peeped up behind the eastern hills. He felt in his pockets for a match. Then he climbed down the pine and broke off dead stubs from its trunk and kindled a small fire. Awaking Lew and Jim, he said, "Time to eat, boys."

He sliced three cuts of meat from the venison saddle and set them to broil over the fire.

"Why, the flood has stopped," Jim said, obviously disappointed."We could have stayed in the cabin loft all night."

"To hear you talk, one would think you wanted to see everything washed out," said Charlie. "After we eat, you can climb down on the roof and exercise a bit. I'm going to sleep now. And you both watch the water mark. I think it has started to drop, but my eyes are all bunged up from staying awake so long."

Lew and Jim picked out a knot on the pine trunk which just showed above the flood. They watched it closely for an hour and found that if the water was not receding, at least it wasn't climbing. Jim clambered down on the roof and watched the enormous chunks of ice and snow float by. It was a wonderful yet terrifying sight to see the entire valley flooded with dirty, sullen water.

"Those hills must be swarming with game," said Lew. "The rats and mink can stick to the river, but coon and possum and skunk, to say nothing of the rabbit and squirrel, must have dry land. There'd be some awful good shooting down there right now."

"Look," called Jim, pointing. A rat swam quietly through the dirty scum with a clean-cut ripple following. "Hand me the rifle," he called. "We can shoot if we can't trap."

But Lew decided to take the shot himself, and just as he aimed, he saw another larger, stronger ripple bearing swiftly down upon the rat. "A mink," he whispered under his breath and fired. Just as Lew pulled the trigger, the rat saw the pursuer and started to dive, but the bullet caught it squarely in the head. Lew turned the rifle on the mink and completed a double; both animals floated around in the quiet eddy behind the cabin.

Jim found a long stick and finally pulled them in. Charlie awoke at noon and broiled more deer steak. Suddenly, Jim yelled, "It's going down! The water's going down!"

They all looked at the knot which had marked the flood height early in the morning. Sure enough, it was two inches above the top wave. It was receding slowly but surely. Charlie sighed with relief. There had been too much happening the last week.

"You'll have to give up your hopes of being Robinson Crusoe," he told Jim. "We can move back in the cabin tomorrow, and there will be heaps and heaps of work to do. The cabin must be cleaned out and dried. This venison will spoil if we don't dry or jerk it, and I'll have to pack a load of flour and sugar over Hog Back Trail from the Ranch. Believe me, there's a full week coming."

The flood was receding fast by night. Charlie decided it would be perfectly safe to spread their beds in the cabin loft. In the morning, they found the cabin free of water and the sun shining brightly. They flung open the doors and windows to dry out the interior. The furs were repacked in the shed.

Charlie stretched and declared. "I feel like old Noah must have when he saw the flood backing away."

They cleaned the trash from the cabin. A huge roaring fire helped dry the floor, and Jim came dancing out of one room. "Look," he cried, holding up a husky river trout in his hands. "Dinner!" It had been carried in with the flood and then trapped when the water drained back into the river.

"We still must jerk those deer saddles," Charlie replied.

So he split the meat into strips half an inch thick and rubbed them with salt and pepper. A drying rack was constructed, merely four stakes driven to form a square with two poles laid across the tops for sills. The strips of venison were threaded on half-inch hickory sticks and laid across the sills. Charlie built a low fire under the meat and ordered Jim to watch it continually, smothering any sudden blaze with wet earth and piling on just enough wood to keep up a smoldering heat.

"How long will it take?" asked Jim.

"About twenty hours," came the answer. "But we will let the fire die down tonight and finish the drying tomorrow. The meat must be hard and brittle and lose at least half its weight before it's jerked."

The cabin was soon dry enough to live in. The fireplace was a big aid in driving out the moisture, and Charlie hunted wood most of the day to keep the fire blazing.

The following morning, he started out to salvage as many traps as he could. The fur season was about over. The flood had doubtless drowned and washed away hundreds of animals, and Charlie determined to leave any survivors to restock the valley. He and Jim hunted and carried home steel traps for two days. They counted up and found only about a fifth gone.

Jim went out in the hills each morning to hunt rabbits and squirrels, but they couldn't live on meat alone. Charlie started over Hog Back Trail to the ranch for a pack load of supplies.

While Charlie was gone, Lew directed Jim to nail down the roof shingles tight. "Don't want another lynx getting this jerked venison," he said. It was hanging close to the rock chimney, where it continued to dry.

Two days later, Charlie brought back a load of baking powder, a small sack of flour, sugar and dried fruit. He was pretty well exhausted from the trip, for he had pushed along steadily with a heavy pack.

"Well," he said as they sat about the fire that night, "this weather pretty much ends trapping season. Can't say we suffered any from monotony."

"No," answered Lew, "I think we managed to keep things moving."

"Now," continued Charlie, "just as soon as the mountain roads dry up, I suggest we pack the skins over to the car we left stored at the ranch and drive up to St. Louis and sell them."

"Suits me," said Lew.

A worried frown gathered on Jim's face. "Are we coming back next winter to trap again?" he asked. Lew eyed him with stern interest.

"The place for a young fellow like you is in school, getting an education and learning to do things that will earn you a heap more money than following the fur trails. You know that's the place you belong right now."

Jim looked downcast. "I suppose so," he confessed.

Lew waxed eloquent then.

"The day is passing when a trapper can step out in the wilderness and make a stake that will keep him over summer. Main reason is there isn't much wilderness left. A young fellow simply must get an education to experience any success in the competition that's growing stronger every year in all the paying professions. Of course, a fellow who likes the woods life can pack out in the timber somewhere, but competition is getting stronger, even out there."

Lew paused for breath and then resumed, "What's going to happen to the old-timers? Charlie and I got lucky with this fur pocket, but look at the trouble we have had already, and it'll only get worse next winter, when word of our catch travels around. Can two husky young fellows afford to camp in the mountains a whole year for about a thousand dollars apiece? Gosh, a bricklayer makes that much in three months!"

"Don't worry the boy, Lew," interposed Charlie. "This year out of school hasn't hurt him any. In fact, I think he has learned a lot more than he would have from books. He's learned to be self-reliant, to have confidence in his own efforts, and that is the biggest lesson in life."

"Then, we won't trap anymore?" faltered Jim.

Charlie looked disapprovingly at his partner.

"Of course we will," he answered heartily. "We'll settle that next fall. What Lew meant was a trapper can't depend upon his catch alone to make a stake. He must run all the outdoor lines. We've got a nice stream for pearling here. The hills grow medical roots, and if we push right along all summer, we'll have a nice little balance on the right side of the ledger. I think, though, the place for you, next fall, is back in school. When we sell our furs, I'm going to hunt up your father and talk things over."

"I don't need any more schooling," protested Jim.

"Don't contradict your Uncle Lew," replied that worthy. "Suppose you shipped a nice bunch of furs to the wholesale market. Those fellows had been quoting extra large skunks at five dollars and you sent a dozen ordinary large ones. Now you figure out what your stuff would bring in cash. I guess I can prove how bad you need an education."

"Don't kid the boy," put in Charlie. "That's a riddle only a fur buyer can solve, and then, ten times out of eleven, the answer won't please the trapper."

"Anyway," said Lew, "next fall and school are both a long ways off, and we do have a couple of thousand dollars' worth of fur here. Charlie and I've been talking about a Western trip after we stop to sell in St. Louis. How'd you like to go with us out on the plains where they still ride saddle horses, rope cattle, and stir up clouds of dust whooping down the street waving six-shooters? Might even get to trap coyotes and shoot rattlesnakes."

Jim, AKA the Skagway Kid, jumped straight up at that, pumped a fist in the air and shouted, "Let's go now!"

(The End)